A NEW HOPE

Ryder Windham

Based on the screenplay by
George Lucas

EGMONT
We bring stories to life

EGMONT
We bring stories to life

First published in Great Britain 2017
by Egmont UK Limited, The Yellow Building,
1 Nicholas Road, London W11 4AN

ISBN 978 1 4052 8542 1
66773/2

Printed in UK

Cover design by Richie Hull

To find more great *Star Wars* books, visit
www.egmont.co.uk/starwars

A long time ago in a galaxy far,
far away. . . .

It is a period of civil war.
Rebel spaceships, striking
from a hidden base, have won
their first victory against
the evil Galactic Empire.

During the battle, rebel
spies managed to steal secret
plans to the Empire's
ultimate weapon, the DEATH
STAR, an armoured space
station with enough power
to destroy an entire planet.

Pursued by the Empire's
sinister agents, Princess
Leia races home aboard her
starship, custodian of the
stolen plans that can save her
people and restore
freedom to the galaxy . . . .

PROLOGUE

THE Clone Wars were over, leaving entire civilisations in ruin. The Jedi Knights were all but extinct. And the Old Republic – the democratic galactic government that had prevailed for a thousand years – had been replaced by the Galactic Empire.

Yet the Empire's supreme ruler, the evil Emperor Palpatine, remained hungry for even more power. To expand his rule, and crush all remnants of the Old Republic, Palpatine had approved the construction of a secret weapon: the Death Star, an immense armoured space station that could destroy an entire planet.

The Empire was not without opposition. The Alliance to Restore the Republic – commonly known as the Rebel Alliance – led the fight to overturn the Empire and bring justice and freedom back to the galaxy.

After rebel spies learned of the Death Star project, they managed to steal a copy of the space station's technical data. The rebels hoped the data would reveal a way to destroy the Death Star. The Empire was determined to recover the stolen plans . . . now in the possession of a young Senator from the planet Alderaan, Princess Leia Organa . . .

CHAPTER 1

BURSTS of laserfire streaked after the consular starship *Tantive IV*, which was racing for the planet Tatooine. The ship was fleeing from the *Devastator*, an immense Imperial Star Destroyer that was firing nearly all its turbolasers at its elusive target. Both vessels had just entered Tatooine's orbit when the *Devastator*'s lasers scored a direct hit on the *Tantive IV*'s primary sensor array. The array exploded, and the blast overloaded the starboard shield projector – which caused another explosion, damaging the power generator system and triggering a chain reaction throughout the ship. With no starboard shield and no power to its engines, the *Tantive IV* was effectively crippled.

Inside the battered *Tantive IV*, the crew raced to extinguish fires as more blasts rocked the ship. Struggling to remain on their feet, rebel crewmen and troops ran through a narrow white-walled passageway, taking little notice of the two robots that stumbled along with them. The droids were C-3PO, a gold-plated humanoid protocol droid, and his counterpart R2-D2, an astromech with a domed head and cylindrical body who moved on three legs.

"Did you hear that?" C-3PO said to R2-D2 as the *Tantive IV*'s engines powered down. "They've shut down the main reactor. We'll be destroyed for sure. This is madness!"

More rebel troops ran into the main corridor. The two droids stepped aside into a shallow alcove to avoid being trampled. The rebels took up defensive positions and aimed their weapons at a sealed hatch at the end of the corridor.

C-3PO said, "We're doomed!"

R2-D2 replied with a series of beeps and whistles.

"There'll be no escape for the princess this time," C-3PO said just loud enough for R2-D2 to hear.

The corridor was suddenly filled with the echoing sounds of metallic latches, clanking and moving around the ship's outer hull. Hearing the noise, C-3PO asked, "What's that?"

R2-D2 beeped nervously. The astromech suspected that the Star Destroyer had used a tractor beam to draw the *Tantive IV* into the Destroyer's main hangar, and the clanking sounds were produced by a magnetic paralysing pincer lock as it secured the captured ship. Indeed, that was exactly what had happened: the *Tantive IV* was now nestled in the Star Destroyer's underside hangar. Although the hangar remained exposed to space, the *Tantive IV* was trapped like a small fish in a sando aqua monster's belly.

Inside the *Tantive IV*'s corridor, the droids braced themselves against the alcove wall as the rebel troops kept their eyes on the sealed hatch. Suddenly, sparks blazed at the hatch's frame as it was cut from the other side. Then the hatch exploded. Before the smoke cleared, a white-armoured Imperial stormtrooper stepped through the shattered hatch and fired his blaster rifle at the rebels. The stormtrooper was immediately cut down by a hail of return fire from the rebels, but another stormtrooper appeared from behind him, firing as he stepped over his fallen predecessor. The second stormtrooper also fell to the rebels, but there were more where he came from, and they kept on coming.

The stormtroopers were identical. Each wore a head-concealing white helmet that resembled a robotic face, with black polarised lenses for eyes and a grimacing vocoder for the mouth. Below the vocoder, jutting out from the helmet's chin, a grilled breathing filter was set between two artificial air-supply nozzles.

More stormtroopers poured into the main corridor. From their alcove, the droids watched helplessly as several rebel soldiers were shot down. The rebels fought back, and the corridor was filled with deadly, criss-crossing projectiles. When a laserbolt slammed into the wall near the droids, R2-D2 responded with a loud electronic shriek, then rolled forward on his treads. Not wanting to be left behind, C-3PO stepped after his companion. Laserbolts whizzed past their forms as the droids crossed the narrow corridor to a hatch that faced the alcove. Incredibly, neither droid was hit during their quick but harrowing exit.

Overwhelmed, the surviving rebels retreated hastily to other parts of the *Tantive IV.* A squad of stormtroopers secured the corridor, then instinctively moved away from the hatch as a tall, caped figure entered. He was clad entirely in black, giving him the appearance of a menacing shadow amidst the white-armoured stormtroopers in the white-walled passageway. His head was concealed by a helmet with a fierce-looking faceplate, distinguished by two recessed black oval visual sensors positioned above a triangular respirator. A life-support-system control panel was affixed to his chestplate, and he carried with him the sound of his mechanical, laboured breathing. Everything in his outward appearance suggested that the black-armoured suit only barely contained the evil lurking within.

He was Darth Vader, the Sith Lord.

Darth Vader ignored the two dead stormtroopers near the exploded hatch and surveyed the fallen rebels on the corridor floor. He felt neither pity nor remorse for the lives that had been extinguished.

These men brought this upon themselves. They sealed their fate the day they chose to oppose the Empire.

Stepping over the corpses, Darth Vader proceeded into the *Tantive IV*.

R2-D2 stood in a dimly illuminated subhallway that linked the *Tantive IV*'s port airlock to the escape pod access tunnel. He had lost sight of C-3PO almost immediately after they'd made their hasty exit from the main corridor, and assumed the golden droid had either got lost or found a good hiding place. The only reason R2-D2 had not yet attempted to find C-3PO was because he was busy making a holographic recording of Princess Leia Organa.

R2-D2 had run into the young woman as she hid in the subhallway. She had fair skin, dark brown hair, and wore a loose-fitting white gown and travel boots. She sounded distressed as she spoke, which was understandable, given the circumstances. The droid was still recording when she glanced at a hatch behind her, then turned back and bent to insert a data card into the slot beneath R2-D2's radar eye. The droid stopped recording.

From nearby, C-3PO cried, "Artoo, where are you?"

While Leia crept off to hide against the nearby wall,

R2-D2 extended his retractable third leg to the floor and moved in the direction of C-3PO's voice.

"At last!" C-3PO said when he saw R2-D2. "Where have you been? They're heading in this direction. What are we going to do? We'll be sent to the spice mines of Kessel or smashed into who knows what!"

R2-D2 rolled away from C-3PO, heading for the escape pod access tunnel.

"Wait a minute," C-3PO said. "Where are you going?"

Princess Leia peeked out from her hiding place and watched the droids exit. She thought, *Unless that R2 unit delivers my message, all will be lost!*

As stormtroopers and captured rebel troops marched by, Darth Vader stood in the consular ship's operations forum and wrapped his black-gloved fingers around the neck of its commanding officer, Captain Antilles. Vader was about to proceed with his interrogation when a stormtrooper rushed up and announced, "The Death Star plans are not in the main computer."

Vader turned his visor to gaze at Captain Antilles. "Where are those transmissions you intercepted?" the Sith Lord asked as he lifted Antilles off the floor. "What have you done with those plans?"

Antilles gasped, "We intercepted no transmissions. *Aaah* . . . this is a consular ship. We're on a diplomatic mission."

Tightening his grip, Vader asked, "If this is a consular ship . . . where is the ambassador?"

When no answer came from Antilles, Vader decided the interrogation was over. There was a horrid snapping sound from Antilles' neck, then his body went limp. Vader tossed the dead soldier against the wall, then turned to a stormtrooper.

"Commander," Vader ordered, "tear this ship apart until you've found those plans and bring me the passengers. I want them alive!"

The stormtroopers marched off to search the ship.

Soon, a squad arrived at the shadowy port subhallway and moved quietly down its length. It didn't take long for a stormtrooper to spot Princess Leia's white gown against the dark-walled chamber.

"There's one!" the stormtrooper shouted as he raised his blaster rifle. "Set for stun!"

Leia stepped out from her hiding place, raised her laser pistol, and fired at the nearest stormtrooper. Her blaster was not set on stun, and the fired bolt punched through her target's armour, dropping him instantly. Leia turned to run but another stormtrooper fired a paralysing ray at her back.

The princess was hit and went sprawling to the floor.

The stormtrooper squad stepped over to inspect Leia's inert body. "She'll be all right," said the squad's leader. "Inform Lord Vader we have a prisoner."

✦

The sound of blasterfire from the subhallway reached C-3PO as he followed R2-D2 through the adjoining escape pod access tunnel. C-3PO had thought R2-D2 was heading for the next chamber, so he was surprised when he saw the astromech stop, turn and open the hatch to an escape pod.

"Hey, you're not permitted in there," C-3PO said. "It's restricted. You'll be deactivated for sure."

R2-D2 moved into the pod and beeped back at the golden droid.

"Don't you call me a mindless philosopher, you overweight glob of grease!" C-3PO retorted. "Now come out before somebody sees you."

R2-D2 remained in the pod and whistled at C-3PO.

"Secret mission?" C-3PO asked, baffled. "What plans? What are you talking about? I'm not getting in there!"

Yet another explosion rocked the ship, violently rattling C-3PO's metal joints. Without further hesitation, the golden droid stumbled through the open hatch and into the pod. He said, "I'm going to regret this."

The hatch snapped shut behind the droids. Then there was a muffled explosion as the pod's latches blew away and the pod ejected from the *Tantive IV*. The pod's rocket engines propelled it out of the Star Destroyer's open hangar and into space.

The ejected pod did not go unnoticed by the

Imperials. On board the *Devastator*, the chief pilot saw the pod's image streak across his main viewscreen, and said, "There goes another one."

But the *Devastator*'s captain had already checked his sensor scopes and ordered, "Hold your fire. There's no life-forms. It must have short-circuited."

The escape pod continued to plummet away from the Star Destroyer. Inside, C-3PO peered through the small circular window that was the vessel's single viewport. Gazing back at the rapidly receding view of the *Tantive IV* within the Star Destroyer's main hangar, he commented, "That's funny, the damage doesn't look as bad from out here."

R2-D2 beeped an assuring response.

"Are you sure this thing is safe?" C-3PO said, unconvinced.

Soon, even the Star Destroyer was just a distant speck from the droids' perspective. And the escape pod kept falling, all the way to the harsh surface of the planet below.

CHAPTER 2

AFTER the stormtroopers revived Princess Leia, they placed binders on her wrists and escorted her through the *Tantive IV*. Leia could not help but notice that the white-walled corridors were now scorched and the air was heavy with the scent of blaster fumes.

Darth Vader and a black-uniformed Imperial officer stepped out through an open hatch and entered the corridor in front of the stormtroopers and Leia. The stormtroopers stopped walking, and Leia faced the Sith Lord.

"Darth Vader," Leia said. "Only you could be so bold. The Imperial Senate will not sit still for this. When they hear you've attacked a diplomatic –"

"Don't act so surprised, Your Highness," Vader interrupted. "You weren't on any mercy mission this time. Several transmissions were beamed to this ship by rebel spies. I want to know what happened to the plans they sent you."

"I don't know what you're talking about," Leia said, feigning innocence. "I'm a member of the Imperial Senate on a diplomatic mission to Alderaan . . ."

"You are a part of the Rebel Alliance . . . and a traitor," Vader snarled. "Take her away!"

As the stormtroopers led Leia out of the consular ship to the Star Destroyer, Vader and the black-uniformed officer turned to continue their inspection of the rebel ship. The officer said, "Holding her is dangerous. If word of this gets out, it could generate sympathy for the Rebellion in the Senate."

"I have traced the rebel spies to her," Vader said. "Now she is my only link to finding their secret base."

Walking faster to keep up with Vader's long strides, the officer added, "She'll die before she'll tell you anything."

"Leave that to me," Vader said. "Send a distress signal and then inform the Senate that all aboard were killed!"

As Vader arrived at a corridor intersection, Imperial Commander Praji stopped him. "Lord Vader, the battle station plans are not aboard this ship! And no transmissions were made. An escape pod was jettisoned during the fighting, but no life-forms were aboard."

Vader seethed. He said, "She must have hidden the plans in the escape pod. Send a detachment down to retrieve them. See to it personally, Commander. There'll be no one to stop us this time."

"Yes, sir," said Commander Praji.

Vader stepped to a viewport and gazed down at the sand planet. From space, it looked just as inhospitable as he knew it was on the surface.

To think I lived there once, that it was my home before the Jedi came and took me away. My mother breathed her last on this world, and for years I felt such . . . agonising loss.

Now I feel nothing. This world means as much to me as a speck of dust, and all its inhabitants might as well be dust, too.

"How did we get into this mess?" C-3PO said. "I really don't know how." He and R2-D2 were trudging down a steep dune, and the sand was already getting into his gears. C-3PO sighed. "We seem to be made to suffer. It's our lot in life."

The droid glanced behind them. His footprints and R2-D2's treadmarks extended all the way back to the landed escape pod, which was still in sight where they'd left it. Had there been a less sandy spot to land on Tatooine, R2-D2 might have steered for it, but since it was a desert world, R2-D2 had only two choices: sandy desert or treacherous rock formations. R2-D2 wisely opted for sand, and beeped at C-3PO to remind him of this, but the golden droid wasn't listening.

"I've got to rest before I fall apart," C-3PO said,

trying to remember the last time he'd had an oil bath. "My joints are almost frozen."

R2-D2 beeped, encouraging C-3PO to keep moving.

C-3PO ignored him again and stopped to look around. There was a rock mesa to his right and sand everywhere else. "What a desolate place this is," he observed.

Tired of being ignored, R2-D2 whistled, made a sharp right turn, then started off in the direction of the rock mesa.

"Where do you think you're going?" C-3PO asked.

R2-D2 answered with a stream of electronic noise.

"Well, I'm not going that way," C-3PO said. "It's much too rocky. This way is much easier."

R2-D2 justified his change of direction with another round of beeps.

"What makes you think there are settlements over there?" C-3PO said.

R2-D2 beeped a very detailed explanation.

"Don't get technical with me," C-3PO chided with annoyance.

The astromech decided it was time to inform C-3PO about his mission, and uttered more beeps and whistles.

"What mission?" C-3PO said, dumbfounded. "What are you talking about? I've just about had enough of you! Go that way! You'll be malfunctioning within a day, you near-sighted scrap pile!" Thoroughly flustered, C-3PO gave a swift kick to R2-D2's right leg, then turned and headed off for the dunes. As he stormed off, he said in a scolding tone, "And don't let me catch you following me begging for help, because you won't get it."

R2-D2 rotated his domed head to see C-3PO walking away from him. He beeped again, trying to convince C-3PO to come with him.

"No more adventures," C-3PO shouted back as he continued walking. "I'm not going that way."

R2-D2 rotated his head to look away from C-3PO's departing figure, then rotated for another look at C-3PO's back. The astromech let out a forlorn, whimpering beep, and waited a moment longer. But when he realised C-3PO was determined to go his own way, R2-D2 turned his dome in the other direction and moved off, heading for the rock mesa.

"That malfunctioning little twerp," C-3PO muttered to himself several hours after parting ways with R2-D2. "This is all his fault! He tricked me into going this way, but he'll do no better."

Tatooine's skies had turned cloudy, but C-3PO could still feel the heat from the planet's two suns. He walked past the skeletal remains of a large, long-necked creature, and trembled at the thought that the deceased might have any living relatives nearby.

C-3PO noticed a metal O-ring was missing from

his left knee joint, and realised it must have jarred loose. He knew there was no chance he'd ever find the disc-shaped piece of metal again. With each step, his sand-clogged gears made horrid grinding sounds. He was ready to give up.

Then he saw something on the horizon.

"Wait, what's that?" he said. It was an angular shape with a winking light. Despite the distance, the droid could tell he was looking at a large vehicle. "A transport! I'm saved!" In his loudest voice, he shouted, "Over here! Hey! Hey!" He continued shouting and waving his arms. "Help! Please, help!"

At first, he felt relief when he saw the transport turn and move in his direction. But when it arrived and C-3PO met the transport's drivers, he wished he'd gone with R2-D2 after all.

As Tatooine's two suns set, the temperature dropped. And from every shadowy hole and crevice that lined the canyon walls, nocturnal animals chirped and croaked and hissed in appreciation of the cool air that came with darkness.

R2-D2 had never been so spooked in his life.

He had already evaded sandpits, traversed circuit-jarring terrain, and boldly descended a high cliff to arrive at the canyon floor. However, these accomplishments had been merely challenges to overcome, and they did not bolster R2-D2's sense of courage. In his experience, dealing with nature was one thing, and dealing with organic creatures was something entirely different, especially when one was a stranger in their territory. Even though his primary photoreceptor was equipped with radar and allowed him to see in the dark, it didn't change the fact that nightfall was – for some large predators – the preferred time for scavenging.

Despite his wariness, R2-D2 kept moving. He was on a mission, and no one could ever call R2-D2 disloyal. And so he rolled forward on his treads, proceeding cautiously through the rock canyon.

A pair of lights flickered between two boulders, then winked off. R2-D2 paused. Using his sensors, the astromech detected a number of life-forms in this area. As he wondered if the lights on his own domed head might have attracted the life-forms, he heard some rocks fall. They were just small rocks, pebbles mostly, but R2-D2 knew that rocks usually didn't fall on their own.

Then he saw a small, dark form dart behind a boulder. R2-D2 couldn't help but emit a whimpering beep. He started moving forward again, hoping that the life-forms would stay where they were and allow him to pass.

Suddenly, a squat, hooded figure with glowing eyes jumped out from the shadows, shouted in an alien language, and fired an ionisation blaster at R2-D2. The astromech shrieked as rippling charges of electricity travelled over and through his body. He didn't stop screaming until the charges crackled and died. Then his dome lights dimmed, and he pitched forward and crashed against the hard ground.

The shooter lowered his blaster. He called out to the surrounding shadows, and seven more hooded figures scurried out from their hiding places. All were short, most no taller than R2-D2 when standing. Like the shooter, they were completely shrouded in dark brown robes made of heavy cloth. Their only visible facial features were their glowing eyes: two bright yellow lights staring out from the darkness of their cloaked heads.

They chittered at one another with delight as they stepped up to examine the fallen droid. The shooter holstered his blaster, then directed his fellows to lift the R2 unit. They picked him up and carried him off to their waiting transport.

The transport was an enormous rust-covered vehicle with a high, sharply angled prow that appeared to cut into the night sky. The transport rested on four massive treads that elevated the hull from the ground. The hooded figures carried the deactivated R2 unit under the transport and set him on his feet, positioning him under an extensible repulsorlift-tube. As the tube was lowered a short distance above the droid's head, one hooded figure quickly welded a restraining bolt to a panel on the front of the droid's cylindrical body. After the restraining bolt was secured, the repulsor switched on, and R2-D2 was sucked up into the transport. Having made their catch, the hooded figures entered the transport via a landing ramp.

R2-D2 reactivated to find himself in a scrap heap in a cramped, low-ceilinged chamber. Durasteel shavings had come to rest upon his head, but they fell away as he leaned away from a metal wall. Pushing various bits of scrap aside, he moved out of the heap, then rotated his dome to study his cluttered surroundings. He was surprised to see an old RA-7 servant droid nearby, seated with his back against a metal wall. The RA-7 gave R2-D2 a dismissive glance.

R2-D2 heard an electronic voice, and turned to face a red R5 astromech against another wall; the R5 rotated its characteristic head - shaped like an inverted cup - in greeting. Then R2-D2 spotted a binocular-eyed Treadwell droid and a box-shaped GNK power droid.

Curious, R2-D2 moved up a narrow aisle to explore the chamber. As he passed an ancient CZ secretary droid that was swaying back and forth amidst a pile of scrap, he heard a familiar voice call out, "Artoo?"

It was C-3PO. The golden droid had been hunched down against a wall, but seeing his friend, he struggled to his feet. "Artoo! It is you!" he cried happily. "It is you!"

R2-D2 beeped in salutation at C-3PO, who also had a restraining bolt secured to his chest. Both droids nearly stumbled when the transport suddenly lurched forward. Under the star-filled sky, the transport chugged off and headed out of the canyon.

The next morning, a squad of Imperial stormtroopers found the abandoned escape pod half buried in the sand. A *Sentinel*-class landing craft had delivered the stormtroopers to Tatooine, where they'd appropriated dewbacks – large four-legged reptiles – from the local authorities. The landing craft lifted away from the escape pod's impact site, leaving the stormtroopers and their dewbacks to search for any sign of the pod's passengers.

In addition to their standard armour and survival gear, the stormtroopers wore pauldrons – protective shoulder armour – over their right shoulders. All the pauldrons were black except for the orange one worn by the squad's captain.

Through the lenses of his stormtrooper helmet, the captain looked from the open pod to the surrounding sand, searching for any signs of passengers. Because of winds and shifting sand, footprints didn't last long on Tatooine, so he considered himself lucky when he spotted the tracks.

"Someone *was* in the pod," he announced to the other stormtroopers. He raised a pair of macrobinoculars to his helmet's lenses and scanned the desert, then added, "The tracks go off in this direction."

Near the Captain, a stormtrooper bent down to lift a shiny metal disk from the sand. Holding it up for inspection, the stormtrooper said, "Look, sir - droids."

"Wake up! Wake up!" C-3PO said to R2-D2 as the transport came to a stop. R2-D2 had switched himself off, but - at C-3PO's urging - his dome's lights activated and he was immediately alert. Other droids were beeping and whirring nervously. Behind the protocol droid, a wide hatch opened and filled the cramped chamber with blinding bright light.

"We're doomed," C-3PO said.

After their reunion, C-3PO had told R2-D2 everything he'd learned about their short, hooded captors since they'd picked him up in the desert. They were Jawas, natives of Tatooine. They scavenged the desert for machinery, which they repaired, utilised and sometimes sold to moisture farmers or other inhabitants. Even their transport - called a sandcrawler - was a scavenged item, a relic from the era of Tatooine's mining boom. The sandcrawler was large enough to serve as a mobile home for an entire clan of Jawas. It was also an autonomous mineral-processing facility, equipped with ore crushers, a superheated smelter, and metal compactors. Being trapped in a vehicle with all these features was more than C-3PO could stand.

Jawas appeared at the open hatch, and a power

droid tried to retreat into the chamber. C-3PO glanced at the Jawas, then back at R2-D2 and said, "Do you think they'll melt us down?"

R2-D2 beeped as a Jawa stepped up behind C-3PO.

"Don't shoot! Don't shoot!" the droid yelped. To R2-D2, he whimpered, "Will this never end?"

The Jawas herded C-3PO, R2-D2 and several other selected droids down the sandcrawler's main ramp. They had arrived at a salt flat, on which stood a domed structure and an evenly spaced series of five-metre-tall spires. The spires were vaporators, used to extract moisture from Tatooine's arid atmosphere. This place was a moisture farm.

Both R2-D2 and C-3PO had spent time on this same moisture farm before, a long time ago. From the astromech's perspective, the place hadn't changed much, but he refused to let old memories distract him from his current mission. As for the protocol droid, his memory was not what it had once been.

A Jawa nudged C-3PO, guiding him to take his place in line with the other droids beside the sandcrawler. A hulking R1 reactor drone stood to C-3PO's right, and a multi-armed Treadwell to his left. R2-D2 stood between the Treadwell and a red astromech. Beyond the red unit, a dome-bodied armoured LIN mining droid hugged the ground at the end of the line.

Two human males - one old, one young - stepped

out of one of the domed structures and approached the sandcrawler. The elder had grizzled hair and haggard features, and wore a sand-dusted robe over his farm tunic. The young man beside him had blond hair and wore a white tunic with a dark leather utility belt.

At the sight of the humans, most of the Jawas became so anxious that they ran off and hid behind the sandcrawler's treads. The Jawas' leader didn't run, but instead walked directly to the haggard-faced man and gibbered an enthusiastic sales pitch.

"Yeah, all right, fine," the older man said to the Jawa. "Let's go."

They'd only taken a few steps forward when a woman's voice called out, "Luke! Luke!"

The young man, Luke Skywalker, turned and trotted past some fusion generator supply tanks to arrive at the edge of a huge, deep hole. The hole was an open courtyard with arched doors and rounded windows set into its high, mud-packed walls. Owned by the Lars family for two generations, the compound had been Luke's home for as long as he could remember. Luke leaned over the hole's edge and looked down. Two domestic vaporators extended up from the courtyard floor, and near them stood Luke's aunt Beru.

"Luke," Beru called up to him, "tell Uncle, if he gets a translator, be sure it speaks Bocce."

"Doesn't look like we have much of a choice," Luke

said, "but I'll remind him." He turned and trotted back after the old man, his uncle Owen. Owen was looking at the red unit in the droid lineup. The Jawa leader gibbered at Owen, who answered, "Yeah, I'll take that red one."

The Jawa leader yapped a sharp command and the other Jawas scurried out from behind the sandcrawler's treads to dust off the red droid. Then, catching Owen's eye, the Jawa leader made encouraging gestures at the blue-domed R2 unit.

"No, not that one," Owen said, rejecting R2-D2. While Luke inspected the red astromech, Owen stepped past the Treadwell, then stopped to face the golden protocol droid. An almost identical droid had served on the Lars family farm a few decades back, so Owen recognised the model. If Owen had had a curious nature or dwelled on the past, he might have wondered if he were looking at the same droid, but on this day, which followed many hard days, his only interest in droids was whether they would be useful to him on the farm. Giving the golden droid a quick study, he said, "You – I suppose you're programmed for etiquette and protocol?"

"Protocol?" C-3PO said. "Why – it's my primary function, sir. I am well versed in all the customs –"

"I have no need for a protocol droid," Owen said, looking away. The golden droid's voice was vaguely familiar, but in Owen's limited experience, he figured all protocol droids sounded alike.

Thinking fast, C-3PO said, "Of course you haven't, sir – not in an environment such as this – that's why I have been programmed –"

Owen interrupted, "What I really need is a droid who understands the binary language of moisture vaporators."

"Vaporators!" C-3PO said as if it were the most wonderful word in the galaxy. "Sir – my first job was programming binary load lifters . . . very similar to your vaporators in most respects . . ."

"Can you speak Bocce?" Owen asked.

"Of course I can, sir," C-3PO answered with pride. "It's like a second language to me . . . I'm as fluent in –"

"All right; shut up!" Owen indicated the protocol droid to the Jawa and said, "I'll take this one."

"Shutting up, sir," C-3PO muttered.

"Luke!" Owen shouted. Luke ran over. His uncle gestured at the protocol droid and the red unit, then said, "Take these two over to the garage, will you? I want them cleaned up before dinner."

"But I was going into Tosche Station to pick up some power converters . . ." Luke whined.

"You can waste time with your friends when your chores are done," Owen said. "Now, come on, get to it!"

"All right, come on," Luke said to the protocol droid.

C-3PO glanced at R2-D2. The astromech emitted a whimpering whistle.

Luke glanced at the R5, who was getting a final dusting from some Jawas. Luke said, "And the red one, come on."

The red droid hesitated and stayed beside R2-D2, who let out a pathetic beep and began trembling.

"Well, come on, Red," Luke said. "Let's go."

Red rolled after Luke and C-3PO. R2-D2 started shaking so hard that he attracted the attention of a Jawa technician, who turned and zapped the droid with a control box. R2-D2 went suddenly silent and stood still.

Red was still rolling along when its top suddenly exploded, launching small parts all over the ground. As smoke poured upward from its ruptured head, Luke called out, "Uncle Owen . . ."

"Yeah?" Owen answered, turning from his financial transaction with the Jawa leader.

"This Artoo unit has a bad motivator," Luke said, gesturing at the smouldering droid. "Look!"

Owen spun to the Jawa and bellowed, "Hey, what're you trying to push on us?"

C-3PO noticed the Jawa technician had reactivated R2-D2, and that the droid was now practically jumping up and down, trying to attract attention so he wouldn't be left behind. C-3PO tapped Luke's shoulder, then pointed to R2-D2 and said, "Excuse me, sir, but that Artoo unit is in prime condition. A real bargain."

Luke said, "Uncle Owen . . ."

Owen looked away from the Jawa. "Yeah?"

Luke pointed at R2-D2. "What about that one?"

Turning back to the Jawa, Owen said, "What about that blue one? We'll take that one."

A few shy Jawas trudged up to the red unit, then glanced at Luke, waiting for his permission before they hauled off the droid. Luke waved his hand to fan away the smoke that was still coming out of the droid's head, then said, "Yeah, take this away."

C-3PO beamed at R2-D2, then turned to Luke and said, "I'm quite sure you'll be very pleased with that one, sir. He really is in first-class condition. I've worked with him before. Here he comes."

R2-D2 scooted away from the sandcrawler and headed for C-3PO and Luke. Luke said, "OK, let's go." He turned and walked toward the domed structure, the main entrance to the Lars family homestead.

C-3PO moved close to R2-D2 and said in a low voice, "Now, don't you forget this! Why I should stick my neck out for you is quite beyond my capacity!"

The droids followed Luke into the entrance dome – their new home.

CHAPTER 3

"**THANK** the Maker!" C-3PO exclaimed with delight as he descended into a large tub. "This oil bath is going to feel so good. I've got such a bad case of dust contamination, I can barely move!"

C-3PO was with Luke and R2-D2 in the homestead's cluttered garage, which doubled as Luke's workshop. R2-D2 rested on a large battery. Luke sat on a bench, lost in thought as he played with a scale model of a T-16 skyhopper. He owned a real T-16, but he'd ripped its stabiliser while racing with friends through Beggar's Canyon, an ancient riverbed that had once been part of the Mos Espa Podrace circuit. Owen had been so angry with Luke that he'd grounded him for the season.

Another lost season.

"It just isn't fair," Luke said in frustration, tossing the model T-16 onto a table. "Oh, Biggs is right. I'm never gonna get out of here!"

C-3PO had never heard of Biggs, and didn't know

why Luke was so upset, but he said, "Is there anything I might do to help?"

Luke looked at C-3PO, and the sight of the wide-eyed droid made a bit of his anger drain. He said, "Well, not unless you can alter time, speed up the harvest, or teleport me off this rock!"

"I don't think so, sir," C-3PO said. "I'm only a droid and not very knowledgeable about such things. Not on this planet, anyway. As a matter of fact, I'm not even sure which planet I'm on."

"Well, if there's a bright centre to the universe, you're on the planet that it's farthest from."

"I see, sir," C-3PO said, sounding disappointed.

"Uh, you can call me Luke."

"I see, Sir Luke."

Luke grinned. "Just Luke." He knelt beside R2-D2 and began cleaning him.

"Oh!" C-3PO said, realising the time had come for introductions. As he rose from the oil bath, he said, "And I am See-Threepio, Human-Cyborg Relations; and this is my counterpart, Artoo-Detoo."

"Hello," Luke said to R2-D2.

R2-D2 beeped.

Luke was using a chrome pick to scrape several connectors on R2-D2's head. Examining it more closely, Luke said, "You got a lot of carbon scoring here. It looks like you boys have seen a lot of action."

Stepping out of the tub, C-3PO said, "With all we've been through, sometimes I'm amazed we're in as good condition as we are, what with the Rebellion and all."

At the mention of the Rebellion, Luke jumped up and whirled at C-3PO. "You know of the Rebellion against the Empire?"

"That's how we came to be in your service, if you take my meaning, sir."

Luke thought, *This is incredible!* He said, "Have you been in many battles?"

"Several, I think," C-3PO said. "Actually, there's not much to tell. I'm not much more than an interpreter, and not very good at telling stories. Well, not at making them interesting, anyway."

Luke's shoulders sagged. *Even if this droid were a good storyteller, I'm sick and tired of hearing stories about far-off worlds . . . stories that just make me want to leave Tatooine that much sooner.*

Luke hunkered down and went back to work on R2-D2. He felt a small metal fragment stuck in the upper corner of the data slot below the droid's head rotation ring, so he reached for a larger pick. "Well, my little friend," Luke said as he dug into R2-D2's data slot, "you've got something jammed in here real good. Were you on a starcruiser or –"

The fragment broke loose with a snap, causing Luke to fall back to the garage floor. He sat up to see a flickering three-dimensional hologram of a young woman being projected from a lens on R2-D2's dome. Speaking via R2-D2's loudspeaker, the hologram said, *"Help me, Obi-Wan Kenobi. You're my only hope."*

Luke said, "What's this?"

R2-D2 beeped quizzically.

"What is what?!?" C-3PO translated with annoyance. "He asked you a question . . . What is *that*?"

The hologram repeated itself. The woman was dressed in white. She held her arms out, pleading, and said, *"Help me, Obi-Wan Kenobi. You're my only hope."* She glanced back over her right shoulder, then returned her gaze forward and bent her knees, extending her right arm like she was touching something. Luke thought, *Maybe she's switching off the holorecorder?* Then the hologram looped back to where it started: *"Help me, Obi-Wan Kenobi. You're my only hope."*

R2-D2 whistled in surprise.

"Oh, he says it's nothing, sir," C-3PO informed Luke. "Merely a malfunction. Old data. Pay it no mind."

"Who is she?" Luke said in awe. "She's beautiful."

C-3PO said, "I'm afraid I'm not quite sure, sir."

Luke couldn't take his eyes off the flickering image of the woman. The loop continued: *"Help me, Obi-Wan Kenobi. You're my only hope . . ."*

"I think she was a passenger on our last voyage,"

C-3PO allowed. "A person of some importance, sir – I believe. Our captain was attached to –"

"Is there more to this recording?" Luke interrupted.

R2-D2 let out several squeaks.

"Behave yourself, Artoo," C-3PO scolded. "You're going to get us into trouble. It's all right, you can trust him. He's our new master."

R2-D2 whistled and beeped a long message to C-3PO.

C-3PO looked at Luke. "He says that he's the property of Obi-Wan Kenobi, a resident of these parts. And it's a private message for him. Quite frankly, sir, I don't know what he's talking about. Our last master was Captain Antilles, but with all we've been through, this little Artoo unit has become a bit eccentric."

"Obi-Wan Kenobi?" Luke mused. "I wonder if he means old Ben Kenobi?"

"I beg your pardon, sir, but do you know what he's talking about?"

"Well, I don't know anyone named Obi-Wan, but old Ben lives out beyond the Dune Sea. He's kind of a strange old hermit." Luke gazed at the hologram again. "I wonder who she is. It sounds like she's in trouble. I'd better play back the whole thing."

R2-D2 beeped a short message to C-3PO.

"He says the restraining bolt has short-circuited his recording system," C-3PO translated. "He suggests that if you remove the bolt, he might be able to play back the entire recording."

"Hm?" Luke said, so captivated by the hologram that he wasn't entirely listening. *Remove the restraining bolt?* "Oh, yeah, well, I guess you're too small to run away on me if I take this off. OK." He reached for a wedged tool and popped the restraining bolt off R2-D2's side. "There you go."

The hologram immediately disappeared.

"Hey, wait a minute," Luke said. "Where'd she go? Bring her back! Play back the entire message."

R2-D2 beeped innocently.

"'*What message?*'" C-3PO translated with disbelief. He raised a hand and whacked R2-D2's dome. "The one you've just been playing! The one you're carrying inside your rusty innards!"

Before Luke or C-3PO could further question R2-D2, Luke's aunt called from outside the garage. "Luke? Luke!"

Dinnertime already? "All right," Luke answered, "I'll be right there, Aunt Beru."

"I'm sorry, sir," C-3PO said, "but he appears to have picked up a slight flutter."

Luke handed the restraining bolt to C-3PO and said, "Here, see what you can do with him. I'll be right back."

As Luke headed out of the garage, C-3PO faced R2-D2 and snapped, "Just you reconsider playing that message for him."

R2-D2 beeped.

"No, I don't think he likes you at all," C-3PO answered, turning away.

R2-D2 beeped again.

"No, I don't like you either."

R2-D2 let out a sad, whimpering beep.

Luke left the garage and crossed the courtyard floor to the dining alcove, a cosy arched-ceiling excavation in the courtyard's wall. His aunt had just put some food in the bowl that was set before his uncle at the head of the table, and she seated herself as Luke walked in.

Luke sat down at the table and said, "You know, I think that Artoo unit we bought might have been stolen."

Owen glowered. "What makes you think that?"

"Well, I stumbled across a recording while I was cleaning him," Luke said, helping himself to the neatly prepared dinner. "He says he belongs to someone called Obi-Wan Kenobi."

Hearing this name, Owen and Beru exchanged a nervous glance, which went unseen by Luke. Chewing his food thoughtfully, he said, "I thought he might have meant old Ben." Looking to his uncle, he asked, "Do you know what he's talking about?"

"Nmm-mm," Owen mumbled, keeping his eyes on the food in his bowl.

"Well, I wonder if he's related to Ben."

"That wizard's just a crazy old man," Owen said. "Tomorrow I want you to take that Artoo unit into Anchorhead and have its memory erased. That'll be the end of it. It belongs to us now."

"But what if this Obi-Wan comes looking for him?"

"He won't," Owen said flatly. "I don't think he exists anymore. He died about the same time as your father."

Luke brightened. "He knew my father?"

"I told you to forget it," Owen snapped. "Your only concern is to prepare those two new droids for tomorrow. In the morning I want them up there on the south ridge working on those condensers."

"Yes, sir," Luke muttered. *Why is Uncle Owen so determined to keep me on the farm?* Knowing better than to argue with his uncle, Luke took a deep breath. "I think those new droids are going to work out fine," he said, doing his best to sound casual. Pushing the food around in his bowl, he continued, "In fact, I, uh, was also thinking about our agreement, about me staying on another season. And if these new droids do work out, I want to transmit my application to the Academy this year."

Owen's eyebrows raised, forming creases across his weather-worn forehead. "You mean the next semester before harvest?"

"Sure," Luke said. "There's more than enough droids."

"Harvest is when I need you the most," Owen said.

"It's only one season more. This year we'll make enough on the harvest that I'll be able to hire some more hands. And then you can go to the Academy next year. You must understand I need you here, Luke."

"But it's a whole 'nother year."

"Look, it's only one more season."

"Yeah," Luke said, rising from the table, "that's what you said last year when Biggs and Tank left."

"Where are you going?" Beru asked, concerned.

"It looks like I'm going nowhere," Luke replied bitterly, stalking past his seated uncle and out of the alcove. "I have to go finish cleaning those droids."

As Luke headed out of the courtyard, Beru looked to her husband. "Owen, he can't stay here forever. Most of his friends have gone. It means so much to him."

"I'll make it up to him next year," Owen said. "I promise."

"Luke's just not a farmer, Owen," Beru said with a sad smile. "He has too much of his father in him."

Owen stared hard at Beru and said, "That's what I'm afraid of."

Luke stepped out of the homestead's entrance dome and kicked at the sand. *It's just not fair!*

He couldn't stop thinking about Biggs Darklighter, his best friend. He'd graduated from the Academy and confided in Luke that he intended to jump ship and join the Rebel Alliance.

I wish I could have left with Biggs. What was it he called Tatooine? "A big hunk of nothing." *Boy, was he ever right. And I'm stuck on it.*

Luke stopped to watch Tatooine's giant twin suns set over a distant dune range. The hot wind tugged at his tunic.

There's no future here. Not for me. But something is out there . . .

The suns sank and vanished beyond the horizon. Luke returned through the entrance dome and proceeded to the garage. It was dark inside and the droids were nowhere in sight. Luke took the droid caller from his utility belt and pressed a button that made a buzzing sound.

"Aah!" C-3PO cried in response to the caller's transmitted shock as he jumped out from his hiding place behind the Lars family landspeeder.

Luke grinned. "What are you doing hiding back there?"

"It wasn't my fault, sir," C-3PO said, his voice trembling. "Please don't deactivate me. I told him not to go, but he's faulty, malfunctioning, kept babbling on about his mission."

"Oh, no!" Luke said, his grin gone. He raced out of the garage.

The sky was already dark and filled with stars when Luke rushed out of the domed entrance. He took his macrobinoculars from his belt and raised them to his eyes, scanning the area for R2-D2.

C-3PO followed Luke onto the salt flat and said, "That Artoo unit has always been a problem. These astrodroids are getting quite out of hand. Even I can't understand their logic at times."

"How could I be so stupid?" Luke said, lowering the macrobinoculars. "He's nowhere in sight. Blast it!"

"Pardon me, sir, but couldn't we go after him?"

"It's too dangerous with all the Sand People around. We'll have to wait until morning."

Just then, Owen's voice called out, "Luke, I'm shutting the power down."

Luke turned and answered, "All right, I'll be there in a few minutes." He turned back for a final glance across the horizon, then muttered, "Boy, am I gonna get it!" Looking to C-3PO, he said, "You know, that little droid is going to cause me a lot of trouble."

Without hesitation, C-3PO replied, "Oh, he excels at that, sir."

CHAPTER 4

OWEN woke up early and went looking for Luke. After calling for him several times from the courtyard, Owen stepped into the kitchen, where Beru was preparing breakfast.

"Have you seen Luke this morning?" Owen asked gruffly.

"He said he had some things to do before he started today, so he left early."

"Uh?" Owen said, watching Beru insert food into a cooking unit. "Did he take those two new droids with him?"

"I think so," Beru said.

Owen looked out the doorway, then grumbled, "Well, he better have those units in the south range repaired by midday or there'll be hell to pay!"

Luke's sand-blasted landspeeder raced over the desert. In the vehicle's open cockpit, C-3PO was behind the controls and Luke sat to his left in the single passenger seat. The landspeeder travelled through the air a mere metre above ground level, and had a top speed of about 250 kilometres per hour. C-3PO didn't think they were traveling nearly that fast, but when he glanced at the speedometer, he wished he hadn't. He'd forgotten how much he disliked high speeds. The sight of low-flying bugs splattered against the speeder's duraplex windshield wasn't pleasant either.

After listening to C-3PO's account of R2-D2 heading for a rock mesa after landing the escape pod in the desert, Luke was fairly certain that the droids had landed in the Dune Sea, and that R2-D2 had been bound for the Jundland Wastes. Luke directed C-3PO to the Wastes, and when they failed to find R2-D2 anywhere on the rock mesa, they steered down into the canyon.

Luke checked the autoscan on the dashboard's scopes. "Look," he said, "there's a droid on the scanner. Dead ahead. Might be our little Artoo unit. Hit the accelerator."

C-3PO did as he was told, increasing thrust from the landspeeder's three turbine engines. Unfortunately, the landspeeder's autoscan failed to detect the presence of Sand People.

Luke and C-3PO found R2-D2 trudging along on

the floor of the massive canyon. C-3PO brought the landspeeder to a stop, then he and Luke left the vehicle and hurried over to R2-D2.

"Hey, whoa!" Luke said. "Just where do you think you're going?"

R2-D2 stopped and offered some feeble beeps.

"Master Luke is your rightful owner now," said C-3PO, angered by R2-D2's response. "We'll have no more of this Obi-Wan Kenobi gibberish . . . and don't talk to me of your mission either. You're fortunate he doesn't blast you into a million pieces right here."

"No, it's all right," Luke said. "But I think we better go."

Suddenly, R2-D2 emitted a flurry of frantic whistles and screams.

Luke looked to C-3PO and asked, "What's wrong with him now?"

C-3PO translated, "There are several creatures approaching from the southeast."

"Sand People!" Luke gasped. "Or worse!" He went to his landspeeder and fetched a laser rifle he'd brought along for the ride. "Come on, let's go have a look."

C-3PO could not remember ever hearing about Sand People. He would not have remembered the fierce nomads by their other name - Tusken Raiders - either. In any event, the golden droid was apprehensive.

Luke repeated, "Come on." The way he said it, he made it sound like there was nothing to worry about.

While R2-D2 remained near the landspeeder, C-3PO followed Luke to climb up behind some nearby boulders that were atop a ridge overlooking the canyon. Luke propped his laser rifle against the boulder that he rested upon, then whipped out his macrobinoculars and peered through them to scan the canyon floor.

Almost immediately he spotted two banthas: large, thick-furred quadrupeds, the beasts of burden to the Tusken Raiders.

"Well, there are two banthas down there," Luke told C-3PO, "but I don't see any . . . Wait a second."

There was a slight movement near the legs of one bantha, then a humanoid figure came into view. The figure was clothed in a gauzy robe, and his head was masked by bandages, distinctive eye-protection lenses and a metal-plated breath filter.

Luke said, "They're Sand People all right. I can see one of them now."

Suddenly, something clouded Luke's field of view, and he lowered his macrobinoculars in time to see that a Tusken Raider had quickly risen to loom directly in front of him. The Tusken Raider roared. C-3PO was so startled that he fell over backward.

The Tusken Raider clutched a gaderffii, a hand-fashioned double-edged axe-like weapon, and held it high over his head. Luke snatched up his laser rifle, but the Tusken Raider swung his gaderffii and cleaved through the rifle's long barrel, knocking Luke to the rock ridge. The Tusken Raider swung at Luke's prone body, but Luke rolled aside to avoid being struck by the gaderffii. The Tusken Raider swung twice again, and Luke dodged those blows too, but the fourth swing connected, and Luke was knocked unconscious.

Below Luke, R2-D2 huddled against the shadows under a rock ledge. The astromech trembled as three Tusken Raiders hauled Luke's unconscious body down to the canyon floor and dumped him unceremoniously beside some rocks near the parked landspeeder. Feeling helpless, R2-D2 watched the Tusken Raiders saunter over to the vehicle. They began to strip it, tossing parts and supplies in all directions. Then they stopped.

A great howling moan echoed through the canyon. Hearing the sound, the three Tusken Raiders fled from the landspeeder. R2-D2 peeked out from the shadows to see the source of the sound: a shuffling humanoid in a dark brown robe with a head-concealing hood. R2-D2 couldn't imagine why the Tusken Raiders were afraid of the approaching life-form, and wondered if perhaps they'd seen something he hadn't.

The hooded figure stopped beside Luke's unconscious form, then bent down and checked his pulse. R2-D2 beeped, and the figured paused. Then he raised a hand to pull back the hood, revealing a bearded old man with thinning white hair.

The man turned to face the R2 unit, then smiled and said, "Hello there! Come here, my little friend. Don't be afraid."

Concerned for Luke, R2-D2 beeped.

"Oh, don't worry, he'll be all right," the man answered.

Luke stirred, then slowly opened his eyes to look up at the old man, who said, "Rest easy, son, you've had a busy day. You're fortunate to be all in one piece."

Luke's eyes widened. "Ben? Ben Kenobi? Boy, am I glad to see you!"

Seeing that all was well, R2-D2 stepped out from under the rock ledge and approached Luke and Ben.

"The Jundland Wastes are not to be travelled lightly," Ben said cheerfully as he helped Luke sit up. "Tell me, young Luke, what brings you out this far?"

"Oh, this little droid!" Luke said, gesturing at R2-D2. "I think he's searching for his former master, but I've never seen such devotion in a droid before . . ."

Ben smiled again at the blue astromech, who beeped at him. Then Ben returned his gaze to Luke, waiting for him to continue.

Luke said, "Ah, he claims to be the property of an Obi-Wan Kenobi. Is he a relative of yours? Do you know who he's talking about?"

Ben's smile was gone. His eyes were on Luke, but

there was something in his expression that seemed simultaneously startled and alert, as if he'd just seen a ghost. Catching his breath, Ben eased himself back to rest against a boulder. "Obi-Wan Kenobi . . ." he said. "Obi-Wan? Now that's a name I've not heard in a long time . . . a long time."

"I think my uncle knows him," Luke said. "He said he was dead . . ."

"Oh, he's not dead," Ben said, smiling as he glanced at the sky. "Not yet."

"You know him?"

"Well, of course I know him. He's me! I haven't gone by the name Obi-Wan since, oh, before you were born."

Luke said, "Well, then, the droid does belong to you."

"Don't seem to remember ever owning a droid," Ben said, eyeing the blue R2 unit more carefully. "Very interesting . . ."

An inhuman barking sound echoed through the canyon. Ben looked up at the overhanging cliffs and said, "I think we better get indoors. The Sand People are easily startled, but they will soon be back. And in greater numbers."

As Ben helped Luke step toward the landspeeder, R2-D2 let out a pathetic beep, causing Luke to remember: "See-Threepio!"

Luke and Ben found the protocol droid sprawled on the rocks near where Luke had been attacked by the Tusken Raider. Wires dangled out from the open socket at C-3PO's left shoulder, and his left arm lay on the ground nearby. The two men lifted the droid to a seated position.

In a dazed voice, C-3PO asked, "Where am I? I must have taken a bad step . . ."

"Well, can you stand?" Luke said. "We've got to get you out of here before the Sand People return."

"I don't think I can make it," C-3PO said. "You go on, Master Luke. There's no sense in you risking yourself on my account. I'm done for."

"No, you're not," Luke said sympathetically. "What kind of talk is that?"

Thinking of the Tusken Raiders, Ben said, "Quickly. They're on the move."

Ben and Luke helped C-3PO to his feet, gathered up his left arm and returned to the landspeeder. Because the speeder had only two seats, the droids were placed atop the vehicle's rear section, on the panels that covered the repulsor field system generator: R2-D2's cylindrical body rested upon the panel behind the passenger seat; C-3PO sat behind the driver's seat and wedged his metal legs down into the open cockpit, between the seats. When the droids were secured, Ben climbed into the passenger seat and directed Luke to drive out of the canyon.

+

Ben's house was a dome-roofed hovel built upon an elevated ridge in the Jundland Wastes. The group had left the landspeeder parked outside, and were in the house's modest living area. The room was cool, clean and minimally furnished, with only a few displayed possessions.

The damage to C-3PO's arm hadn't been serious, so Luke – despite a protest from R2-D2 – had decided to make the repairs himself. After giving Luke a toolbox, Ben had taken a chair beside a low round table. To Ben's right, Luke and C-3PO sat on the edge of his bed, which was set in a concave alcove. R2-D2 stood near a storage chest on the floor and peered over the round table to watch Luke work on C-3PO's arm.

"Tell me, Luke," Ben said. "Do you know about your father's service in the Clone Wars?"

"No, my father didn't fight in the wars," Luke said as he reconnected a wire in C-3PO's arm. "He was a navigator on a spice freighter."

"That's what your uncle told you," Ben said. "He didn't hold with your father's ideals. Thought he should have stayed here and not gotten involved."

Luke turned to face Ben. "You fought in the Clone Wars?"

"Yes. I was once a Jedi Knight, the same as your father."

Luke looked away. "I wish I'd known him."

Ben said, "He was the best star pilot in the galaxy and a cunning warrior." He grinned at Luke. "I understand you've become quite a good pilot yourself." Then a faraway look came over his eyes. He added, "And he was a good friend. Which reminds me . . ."

Ben rose from his seat and walked past R2-D2 to raise the lid on the storage chest. "I have something here for you." He removed a shiny, cylindrical object. "Your father wanted you to have this when you were old enough, but your uncle wouldn't allow it. He feared you might follow old Obi-Wan on some damned-fool idealistic crusade like your father did."

Still seated on the bed, C-3PO turned to Luke and said, "Sir, if you'll not be needing me, I'll close down for a while."

"Sure, go ahead," Luke said.

C-3PO remained seated as he switched himself off. His eyes winked off and his head slumped forward.

Ben handed the shiny object to Luke, who stood and took it in his right hand. Luke asked, "What is it?"

"Your father's lightsaber," Ben said. "This is the weapon of a Jedi Knight. Not as clumsy or random as a blaster."

Luke's fingers found the activation plate, and the blade – a blue beam of pure energy – emitted instantly from an aperture at the end of the handgrip. The weapon made a humming sound. Fascinated, Luke tested the weapon, moving his arm to cut through the air with the glowing blade.

"An elegant weapon for a more civilised age," Ben commented as he returned to his chair. "For over a thousand generations the Jedi Knights were the guardians of peace and justice in the Old Republic. Before the dark times, before the Empire."

Luke deactivated the lightsaber and sat back down on the edge of the bed. Facing Ben, he asked, "How did my father die?"

Ben glanced away from Luke. Choosing his words carefully, he returned his gaze to him and said, "A young Jedi named Darth Vader, who was a pupil of mine until he turned to evil, helped the Empire hunt down and destroy the Jedi Knights. He betrayed and murdered your father."

Luke was stunned. *Why didn't Uncle Owen and Aunt Beru tell me this?*

"Now the Jedi are all but extinct," Ben continued. "Vader was seduced by the dark side of the Force."

"The Force?" Luke said.

"The Force is what gives the Jedi his power," Ben said. "It's an energy field created by all living things. It surrounds us and penetrates us. It binds the galaxy together."

R2-D2 beeped.

Rising again, Ben stepped over to R2-D2 and said,

"Now, let's see if we can't figure out what you are, my little friend. And where you come from."

As Ben touched R2-D2's dome, Luke said, "I saw part of the message he was –"

R2-D2's hologram projector flicked on, and Ben said, "I seem to have found it."

Ben returned to his seat, and R2-D2 projected the flickering hologram of the young woman so that she appeared to be standing upon the table.

"General Kenobi," said the woman's hologram, *"years ago you served my father in the Clone Wars. Now he begs you to help him in his struggle against the Empire. I regret that I am unable to present my father's request to you in person, but my ship has fallen under attack, and I'm afraid my mission to bring you to Alderaan has failed. I have placed information vital to the survival of the Rebellion into the memory systems of this Artoo unit."*

Ben glanced at R2-D2, then back at the hologram.

"My father will know how to retrieve it," the woman's hologram continued. *"You must see this droid safely delivered to him on Alderaan. This is our most desperate hour. Help me, Obi-Wan Kenobi. You're my only hope."*

The woman's hologram glanced over her right shoulder, then bent to adjust something, just as Luke had seen her do before. He now realised she must have turned in response to something or someone behind her, then turned back to manually switch off R2-D2's holorecorder. The hologram flickered off

Ben sat back in his chair and tugged at his beard, thinking hard.

Luke said, "Who is she?"

Ben looked to Luke and said, "You must learn the ways of the Force if you're to come with me to Alderaan."

"Alderaan?" Luke said with disbelief. Rising away from Ben, he added, "I'm not going to Alderaan." He moved toward the door. "I've got to get home. It's late; I'm in for it as it is."

"I need your help, Luke," Ben said. "*She* needs your help. I'm getting too old for this sort of thing."

"I can't get involved!" Luke protested. "I've got work to do! It's not that I like the Empire – I hate it! But there's nothing I can do about it right now. It's such a long way from here."

"That's your uncle talking."

Luke sighed. "Oh, boy, my uncle. How am I ever going to explain this?"

"Learn about the Force, Luke."

Exasperated, Luke said, "Look, I can take you as far as Anchorhead. You can get a transport there to Mos Eisley or wherever you're going."

Ben looked away from Luke and said, "You must do what you feel is right, of course."

What I feel is right? How can he say that? I'd like

to help Ben and . . . her, *whoever she is. But is it right to run out on Uncle Owen and Aunt Beru? They're the only family I've got, and I'm not going to let anything happen to them. If that's not right, then maybe I'd rather be wrong!*

CHAPTER 5

WHILE his squad of stormtroopers continued their search on Tatooine for the Death Star plans, Darth Vader travelled by Star Destroyer to deliver Princess Leia Organa to the Death Star.

The Death Star was, quite simply, the largest space station ever built. Shaped like an orb, it was 120 kilometres in diameter, the size of a Class IV moon. Its quadanium steel outer hull had two prominent features: an equatorial trench and - on its upper hemisphere - a concave superlaser focus lens. The trench contained ion engines, hyperdrives and hangar bays; the superlaser had enough power to annihilate entire worlds.

But despite all its staggering power, at least one person on the Death Star was concerned about the Rebellion.

"Until this battle station is fully operational we are vulnerable," said General Tagge. He was in a conference room, seated at a circular black table with six other high-ranking Imperial officials. Tagge was looking to his right at the seated figure of Admiral Motti, the senior Imperial commander in charge of operations on the Death Star. Tagge continued, "The Rebel Alliance is too well equipped. They're more dangerous than you realise."

Admiral Motti sneered, "Dangerous to your starfleet – not to this battle station!"

But Tagge wasn't finished. "The Rebellion will continue to gain support in the Imperial Senate as long as –"

"The Imperial Senate will no longer be of any concern to us," interrupted a gaunt older man with hollow cheeks who had just walked into the conference room. He was Grand Moff Tarkin, and he entered with Darth Vader at his side. In the Imperial hierarchy, Tarkin reported only to the Emperor.

Vader remained standing while Tarkin took his seat between Admiral Motti and General Tagge. Tarkin continued, "I have just received word that the Emperor has dissolved the council permanently. The last remnants of the Old Republic have been swept away."

"That's impossible," General Tagge said. "How will the Emperor maintain control without the bureaucracy?"

Tarkin said, "The regional governors now have direct control over their territories. Fear will keep the local systems in line. Fear of this battle station."

"And what of the Rebellion?" asked Tagge. "If the rebels have obtained a complete technical readout of this station, it is possible, however unlikely, that they might find a weakness and exploit it."

From beside Tarkin, Darth Vader said, "The plans you refer to will soon be back in our hands."

To Tagge, Admiral Motti promised, "Any attack made by the rebels against this station would be a useless gesture, no matter what technical data they've obtained. This station is now the ultimate power in the universe. I suggest we use it."

Vader warned, "Don't be too proud of this technological terror you've constructed. The ability to destroy a planet is insignificant next to the power of the Force."

Motti sneered and said, "Don't try to frighten us with your sorcerer's ways, Lord Vader. Your sad devotion to that ancient religion has not helped you conjure up the stolen data tapes or given you clairvoyance enough to find the Rebels' hidden fort–"

Suddenly, Motti stopped speaking. Vader never actually touched Motti, but the Dark Lord made a pinching movement with his gloved hand and caused Motti to desperately reach to his own throat. The admiral was choking. His eyes remained fixed on Vader as his body spasmed.

Pinching the air with his fingers, Vader said, "I find your lack of faith disturbing."

Tarkin eyed Vader, then said, "Enough of this! Vader, release him!"

"As you wish," Vader said. He lowered his hand.

Air rushed into Motti's lungs and his head slumped forward. Breathing hard, he stared at the table, then looked up to boldly glare at Vader.

Tarkin said, "This bickering is pointless. Lord Vader will provide us with the location of the rebel fortress by the time this station is operational. We will then crush the Rebellion with one swift stroke."

Luke, Ben and the two droids were speeding through the Jundland Wastes, heading for the community of Anchorhead, when they came upon what was left of the Jawa sandcrawler. Smoke billowed from fires that still burned inside and around the bulky, rusted vehicle. Dozens of Jawas lay dead, their small forms scattered across the sand.

Luke stopped so he and Ben could examine the wreckage. The sandcrawler's hull was riddled with blaster damage, and it appeared the entire Jawa clan had been wiped out.

"It looks like the Sand People did this, all right," Luke said to Ben. "Look, there's gaffi sticks, bantha tracks.

It's just . . . I never heard of them hitting anything this big before."

"They didn't," Ben said. "But we are meant to think they did." Gesturing at the bantha tracks, he continued, "These tracks are side by side. Sand People always ride single file to hide their numbers."

Luke said, "These are the same Jawas that sold us Artoo-Detoo and See-Threepio."

Ben pointed at the scorched dents in the sand-crawler's hull. "And these blast points, too accurate for Sand People. Only Imperial stormtroopers are so precise."

Baffled, Luke asked, "But why would Imperial troops want to slaughter Jawas?" Searching for his answer, he looked at R2-D2 and C-3PO, who stood next to the parked speeder.

The droids, Luke realised. *The stormtroopers want the information in R2-D2!*

Then a more awful realisation hit Luke. He said, "If they traced the robots here, they may have learned who they sold them to, and that would lead them back . . . home!"

Luke bolted for the landspeeder.

"Wait, Luke!" Ben shouted. "It's too dangerous!"

Not heeding Ben's warning, Luke jumped into the landspeeder, punched the ignition and sped away from the burning sandcrawler.

+

Luke saw the rising smoke from kilometres away.

The Lars homestead was consumed by a fiery blaze. Luke's landspeeder was still slowing to a stop when he jumped out. Dense black smoke poured out from the garage roof. He shouted, "Uncle Owen! Aunt Beru! Uncle Owen!"

No response.

Luke didn't know where to look first. Dazed and afraid, he stumbled past debris, hoping to find his uncle and aunt alive. *Maybe they weren't here when the stormtroopers came. Uncle Owen might have gone to check some vaporators . . . but what about Aunt Beru?* The hole that had contained the courtyard now resembled a small volcano, erupting large clouds of grey smoke.

Don't be dead! Luke's mind raced. *Don't be dead don't be dead don't be dead!* His eyes darted to the entrance dome. More fire, more smoke.

Then he saw them.

Two charred, smouldering skeletons, lying in the sand outside the entrance dome.

Luke choked and looked away. Then something inside him snapped, and he forced himself to look back at what the stormtroopers had done to his aunt and uncle.

I'm not afraid. The Empire has taken everything

away from me, but I'm not afraid. Because now I don't have anything to lose.

He stood there, gazing deep into the flames, and felt his anger and determination build.

On the Death Star, two black-uniformed Imperial soldiers preceded Darth Vader down a dark, narrow corridor lined with recessed doorways. All the doors were closed, and behind each was a detention cell. The soldiers stopped in front of one door and it slid up into the ceiling. Darth Vader ducked through the doorway and the two soldiers followed. While the soldiers stood at either side of the open doorway, Vader stepped to the centre of the cramped cell and loomed over the lone prisoner sitting on a bare metal bed that projected from the wall.

Princess Leia.

Darth Vader said, "And now, Your Highness, we will discuss the location of your hidden rebel base."

There was an electronic hum from behind Vader, then a spherical black droid hovered slowly into the cell. A ringed repulsorlift system wrapped around the droid's midsection in such a way that the sphere almost resembled a scale model of the Death Star with its equatorial trench. But unlike the Death Star, which appeared to have a smooth surface from a distance, the droid was festooned with bizarre devices that jutted out at asymmetrical angles. The devices included an electroshock assembly, sonic torture device, chemical syringe and lie determinator.

It was an interrogator droid.

Leia's eyes went wide with fear. The droid extended its syringe and hovered toward her.

The cell door slid closed, and the interrogation began.

Luke drove his landspeeder back to the ruined sandcrawler. In his absence, Ben had prepared a pyre near the sandcrawler, and Luke returned to find C-3PO and R2-D2 placing the Jawa corpses onto the flames. The droids stopped what they were doing and watched Luke as he stepped away from his landspeeder and went to Ben.

Ben saw the torment in his face and said, "There's nothing you could have done, Luke, had you been there. You'd have been killed too, and the droids would now be in the hands of the Empire."

Luke didn't have time for pity. He said, "I want to come with you to Alderaan. There's nothing for me here now. I want to learn the ways of the Force and become a Jedi like my father."

Ben nodded.

When the last Jawa had been placed on the burning pyre, the two men loaded the droids onto the landspeeder and drove off.

En route to the group's destination, Luke had a hard time concentrating. He couldn't stop thinking about his aunt and uncle, and what the Empire had done. After the third time he'd strayed off course, Ben suggested they park the landspeeder and take a moment's pause.

Luke parked on a high, craggy bluff that overlooked a canyon. The droids followed Luke and Ben to the edge of the bluff and gazed out over a wide, haphazard array of runways, landing pads, crater-like docking bays and semi-domed structures that sprawled across the stark canyon floor.

"Mos Eisley spaceport," Ben said. "You will never find a more wretched hive of scum and villainy." Glancing at Luke, he added, "We must be cautious."

Ben and Luke got the droids onto the back of the landspeeder, then the group resumed their journey. This time, Luke stayed on course.

Because Tatooine was in the Outer Rim of space, far from Republic and Imperial activity, Mos Eisley had long been a haven for thieves, smugglers and pirates. Frequent travellers knew better than to stay in town too long. Curious tourists usually wound up wishing they'd stayed at home.

But by any standards, the drive into the city was quite an eyeful. Street traffic consisted of not only landspeeders and swoop bikes but large quadrupeds, including dewbacks and long-necked rontos. Some pedestrians were human, others mechanical, but most were aliens that Luke had never seen before. To resist gawking, he kept his eyes on the road in front of him and steered carefully through the busy streets.

Approaching a congested intersection, Luke slowed the landspeeder to allow some pedestrians to pass. Suddenly, five white-armoured stormtroopers emerged from the sides of the road. All carried blaster rifles. One stormtrooper - the squad leader with an orange pauldron over his right shoulder - waved at Luke, signalling him to pull over. Luke had driven straight into a checkpoint.

The stormtroopers were looking at C-3PO and R2-D2, who were in plain view on the landspeeder's rear section.

Luke felt stupid for not trying to conceal the droids under blankets, then thought, *Could these be the same stormtroopers who killed Uncle Owen, Aunt Beru and the Jawas?* He hadn't expected a confrontation with stormtroopers so soon, and he was unprepared. His heart raced. *One false move and they might open fire. What should I do?* He glanced at Ben, who responded with a reassuring smile. Luke kept both hands on the speeder's steering wheel and looked up at the squad leader.

The stormtrooper asked, "How long have you had these droids?"

"About three or four seasons," Luke lied.

Ben gazed pleasantly at the stormtrooper and said, "They're up for sale if you want them."

Behind Luke, C-3PO trembled. Luke thought, *For sale?! What's Ben talking about?*

The squad leader said, "Let me see your identification."

"You don't need to see his identification," Ben said in a calm, controlled tone.

Looking to his fellow stormtroopers, the squad leader said, "We don't need to see his identification."

Ben said, "These aren't the droids you're looking for."

"These aren't the droids we're looking for," the squad leader repeated.

Luke gave another quick glance at Ben. *He's hypnotising the stormtroopers. But how?*

Ben said to the squad leader, "He can go about his business."

Looking at Luke, the squad leader said, "You can go about your business."

"Move along," Ben said.

"Move along," echoed the squad leader, gesturing with his hand for Luke to proceed. "Move along."

Luke drove the landspeeder away from the stormtroopers, and a few minutes later, Ben directed him to park in front of a run-down blockhouse cantina on the outskirts of the spaceport. The moment the speeder had stopped, a Jawa ran up to run his small hands over the vehicle's hood. As Luke shooed the Jawa away, C-3PO helped R2-D2 off the back of the speeder and muttered, "I can't abide those Jawas. Disgusting creatures."

"Go on, go on," Luke said, waiting for the Jawa to move off. Then he turned to Ben and said, "I can't understand how we got by those troops. I thought we were dead."

Ben said, "The Force can have a strong influence on the weak-minded."

Luke glanced at the cantina and said, "Do you really think we're going to find a pilot here that'll take us to Alderaan?"

"Well, most of the best freighter pilots can be found here," Ben said. "Only, watch your step. This place can be a little rough."

"I'm ready for anything," Luke said as he followed Ben to the cantina's entrance.

CHAPTER 6

C-3PO saw three Jawas loitering in front of the cantina near a large dewback. He turned to the astromech and said, "Come along, Artoo." The droids moved fast to catch up with Luke and Ben.

Luke followed Ben into the cantina's entry lobby. Like most buildings in Mos Eisley, the cantina was essentially a hole in the ground that was covered by a domed roof. Its interior was dark, and the air was filled with thick smoke and fast music. Beyond the entry lobby, a short flight of mud-packed steps descended into a crowded room. A U-shaped bar dominated the room's centre, and the walls were lined by small booths that offered some slight possibility for private conversations. Most of the patrons were aliens, as were the Bith musicians who performed at the bandstand to the right of the bar.

Ben made his way to the bar and immediately struck up a conversation with a human spacer. Luke remained at the top of the steps in the lobby for a moment, overwhelmed by the sight of so many exotic creatures. C-3PO and R2-D2 walked up behind him, then Luke descended the steps. As C-3PO followed him down to the cantina floor, Luke heard a chime from a device in the lobby behind him.

A gruff voice shouted from behind the bar, "Hey, we don't serve their kind here!"

Luke caught sight of the bartender, a dishevelled, middle-aged man with hardened features. The bartender was glaring at him. Confused, Luke said, "What?"

"Your droids," the bartender said. "They'll have to wait outside. We don't want them here."

Luke realised that the chime had sounded from a droid detector. He was also aware of the angry stares from several patrons. Turning to C-3PO, he said, "Listen, why don't you wait out by the speeder. We don't want any trouble."

"I heartily agree with you, sir," C-3PO said. He climbed the steps back to R2-D2, then both made their exit from the building.

Luke glanced back at the bar. Ben was still with the spacer, who appeared to be making introductions with a Wookiee, a hulking, fur-covered alien. An ammunition bandolier was wrapped around the Wookiee's shaggy torso, and a plasma-powered bowcaster was slung over one arm. Luke guessed the Wookiee's height at around 2.25 metres, maybe more.

The spacer moved off, but Ben continued talking with the Wookiee. Luke stepped up to the bar so Ben and the Wookiee were to his right. Luke tried to look casual. *I'll just stand here and watch Ben's back.*

Luke reached across the bar to tug at the bartender's sleeve. The bartender turned his battered face to him with a scowl. Luke ordered a small cup of water. The bartender gave it to him.

Luke took furtive glances at the various spacers and aliens: a pair of Duros leaning against a wall, a white-furred Talz with a small Chadra-Fan, an Ithorian sitting in a corner . . . *I've never seen so many non-humans in one place.*

Somebody on his left shoved him hard.

Luke whirled to face a tusked humanoid alien with bulbous black eyes. The alien spat out, "*Negola dewaghi wooldugger?!?*"

Luke looked away from the alien. *If I ignore him, maybe he'll just go away.*

Luke felt a blunt finger tapping his left shoulder. He turned, expecting to see the tusked alien, but instead he confronted a ghastly-looking man. The man's right eye was blinded and the flesh around it was severely scarred. His nose looked as if it had barely survived an unfortunate encounter with a meat shredder. Gesturing at the tusked alien beside him, the man leaned in close to Luke and said, "He doesn't like you."

The man's breath was foul. Not knowing how else to respond, Luke mumbled, "I'm sorry."

"I don't like you either," said the man with the hideous face. "You just watch yourself. We're wanted men. I have the death sentence on twelve systems."

Luke replied, "I'll be careful."

The man seized Luke's arm and snarled, "You'll be dead."

Luke was still being gripped tightly when Ben turned to face Luke's antagonists. Ben said calmly, "This little one's not worth the effort. Come, let me get you something." Behind Ben, the Wookiee just stood back and watched, waiting to see how the situation would play out.

The man with the disfigured face moved with alarming speed and strength, flinging Luke away from the bar. As Luke crashed into a nearby table, his attackers reached for their blaster pistols.

"No blasters! No blasters!" the bartender shouted too late as he dropped behind the bar.

Luke looked up from where he was sprawled on the floor and saw Ben's hand dart to his belt and draw a lightsaber. The blade flashed on and swept past the blaster-wielding criminals. The disfigured man fell back against the bar, a deep slash across his chest. The tusked alien screamed and his right arm – now severed at the elbow – fell to the floor, still clutching the alien's blaster.

The entire fight had lasted only a matter of seconds. Luke hadn't noticed just when the band had stopped playing, but he was suddenly aware that everyone had gone silent, and the only sound in the cantina was the hum of Ben's lightsaber. Ben maintained his position, holding his lightsaber out from his body as he stared at his two defeated opponents. He glanced out across the room. If anyone else had been looking for a fight, the look in Ben's eyes was enough to discourage them.

Ben deactivated his lightsaber. Almost immediately, the band started playing again, and the patrons went back to their drinks and conversations. It was business as usual again in the Mos Eisley cantina.

The Wookiee followed Ben over to Luke. Ben reached down for Luke's hand to help him up from the floor. Luke said, "I'm all right."

Ben nodded at the Wookiee and told Luke, "Chewbacca here is first mate on a ship that might suit us."

Luke tilted his head back to look up at the Wookiee. *He's definitely more than 2.25 metres.*

Outside the cantina, R2-D2 and C-3PO were standing near Luke's parked landspeeder when they saw the stormtrooper squad marching up the street. Then they saw a man walk quickly out of the cantina. The man stopped the stormtroopers and began talking to the squad leader. The man was very animated, and he kept pointing at the cantina as he described the fight he'd just seen.

C-3PO moved closer to R2-D2 and said, "I don't like the look of this."

Inside the cantina, Chewbacca had guided Ben and Luke to a booth that had a circular table with a cylindrical light at its centre. The booth was against the wall opposite the band, so they would be able to converse without shouting. The booth also offered a clear view of the entry lobby. Chewbacca sat with his back to the wall so he could watch. Ben and Luke sat with their backs to the bar and faced Chewbacca.

They were soon joined by a tall, lean man with dark hair who wore a white shirt with a black vest, trousers and boots. As he moved past the table, Luke noticed the man had a blaster pistol in a quick-draw holster against his right thigh.

The man sat down beside Chewbacca and introduced himself. "Han Solo. I'm captain of the *Millennium Falcon*. Chewie here tells me you're looking for passage to the Alderaan system."

"Yes, indeed," Ben said. "If it's a fast ship."

"Fast ship?" Han said, sounding a bit insulted. "You've never heard of the *Millennium Falcon*?"

Ben asked, "Should I have?"

Han bragged, "It's the ship that made the Kessel run in less than twelve parsecs!"

Ben was not impressed with what he heard as obvious misinformation, and gave Han a look that said so.

Han continued, "I've outrun Imperial starships, not the local bulk cruisers, mind you. I'm talking about the big Corellian ships now. She's fast enough for you, old man. What's the cargo?"

"Only passengers," Ben said. "Myself, the boy, two droids and *no questions asked*."

Han grinned. "What is it? Some kind of local trouble?"

Ben said, "Let's just say we'd like to avoid any Imperial entanglements."

Han let that hang in the air for a moment, then said, "Well, that's the real trick, isn't it? And it's going to cost you something extra." He glanced at Luke. "Ten thousand, all in advance."

"*Ten thousand?*" Luke gasped. "We could almost buy our own ship for that!"

Han lifted his eyebrows. "But who's going to fly it, kid? You?"

"You bet I could," Luke said angrily. "I'm not such a

bad pilot myself!" He looked to Ben and started to rise. "We don't have to sit here and listen –"

Ben touched Luke's arm, urging him to remain seated. Then he returned his gaze to Solo and said, "We can pay you two thousand now, plus fifteen when we reach Alderaan."

Han did the math. "Seventeen, huh?" He thought about it for a few seconds, keeping his eyes on Ben and Luke, then said, "OK. You guys got yourselves a ship. We'll leave as soon as you're ready. Docking Bay Ninety-four."

"Ninety-four," Ben repeated.

Han looked past Ben to the bar and said, "Looks like somebody's beginning to take an interest in your handiwork."

Luke glanced over his shoulder and saw that stormtroopers were talking to the bartender, who was pointing at their booth. The stormtroopers' squad leader said to the bartender, "All right, we'll check it out."

Cantina patrons stepped aside as the stormtroopers walked over to the booth that the bartender had indicated. But when the stormtroopers arrived at the booth, only Han and Chewbacca were seated at the circular table. The stormtroopers glanced at the man and Wookiee, then moved past.

When the stormtroopers were out of earshot, Han smiled at Chewbacca. "Seventeen thousand!" he said.

"Those guys must really be desperate. This could really save my neck. Get back to the ship and get her ready."

Chewbacca headed for the exit. Han stayed at the cantina to finish his drink and settle their tab.

Luke and Ben slipped out the cantina's back door. Ben raised his hood to cover his head as they walked away from the building and tried to lose themselves amidst the pedestrian traffic.

Ben said, "You'll have to sell your speeder."

"That's OK," Luke said. "I'm never coming back to this planet again."

Han Solo was stepping away from his booth at the cantina when he came face-to-face with a green-skinned Rodian aiming a blaster at him.

Speaking through his short trunk, the Rodian said, "Going somewhere, Solo?" The Rodian pushed the blaster's barrel against Han's chest, forcing him to move back to the booth.

"Yeah, Greedo," Han said as he took a seat so that his back was to the wall and the table was directly in front of him. "As a matter of fact, I was just going to see your boss. Tell Jabba that I've got his money."

"It's too late," Greedo said, after seating himself at the other side of the table. Keeping his blaster trained on Solo, he continued, "You should have paid him when you had the chance. Jabba's put a price on your head so large, every bounty hunter in the galaxy will be looking for you. I'm lucky I found you first."

"Yeah, but this time, I've got the money," Han said, slouching back to rest his left knee against the table.

"If you give it to me, I might forget I found you."

"I don't have it *with* me." Han appeared to notice something on the wall to his left, and casually reached up to pick at it with his left hand. This movement distracted the Rodian from noticing the slight shift of Han's other shoulder, as his right hand – below the table, unseen by Greedo – crept to his holstered blaster. Han continued, "Tell Jabba –"

"Jabba's through with you," Greedo interrupted. "He has no time for smugglers who drop their shipments at the first sign of an Imperial cruiser."

"Even *I* get boarded sometimes," Solo said as his right hand eased his blaster out of its holster. "Do you think I had a choice?"

"You can tell that to Jabba. He may only take your ship."

Han's expression became deadly serious. "Over my dead body."

"That's the idea." Greedo chuckled. "I've been looking forward to this for a long time."

"Yes, I'll bet you have."

No one at the bar saw what happened next, but all

heads turned to Han's booth in response to a blinding flash of light and the loud report of blasterfire. Cantina patrons and the bartender saw Han seated across from Greedo, a smouldering hole in the centre of the table between them; the flash had come from the explosion of Greedo's blaster, its shattered remnants still clutched in his long-fingered hand. Greedo's blaster had been destroyed by the same laserbolt – fired by Han – that had torn up through the table. A few sharp-eyed beings also noticed a fresh scorch mark on the wall to the left of Solo's head, which indicated that Greedo might have squeezed off at least one shot. Before anyone could question the outcome of the blaster-fight, Greedo's body slumped forward, collapsing dead upon the table's surface.

Some of the cantina's more monstrous patrons actually enjoyed the smell of fried Rodian.

Han rose from the table and holstered his blaster. As he walked past the bar, heading for the exit, he tossed some coins to the gaping bartender and said, "Sorry about the mess."

In the control room on the Death Star, Darth Vader and Grand Moff Tarkin conferred with Commander Tagge about the interrogation of the captured princess. Vader said, "Her resistance to the mind probe is considerable.

It will be some time before we can extract any information from her."

Admiral Motti approached Tarkin and reported, "The final checkout is completed. All systems are operational. What course shall we set?"

Tarkin looked to Vader and said, "Perhaps she would respond to an alternative form of persuasion."

"What do you mean?" asked Vader.

Tarkin said, "I think it is time we demonstrated the full power of this station." He turned to Motti and commanded, "Set your course for Alderaan."

Motti smiled evilly as he answered, "With pleasure."

CHAPTER 7

"LOCK the door, Artoo," C-3PO said. The two droids were standing in an open doorway in an alleyway near the Mos Eisley cantina. They'd been waiting for Luke and Ben to return and had ducked into the doorway to avoid being seen by an approaching group of stormtroopers.

R2-D2 extended his manipulator arm to the door's locking mechanism and gave it a twist. The door slid shut just in time.

A small Imperial patrol droid hovered up the alley, preceding the stormtroopers. The stormtrooper squad leader said, "All right, check this side of the street." After another trooper checked the door that concealed the two droids, the squad leader said, "The door's locked. Move on to the next one." The stormtroopers followed the patrol droid deeper into the alley.

R2-D2 opened the door and C-3PO peeked out. The golden droid said, "I would much rather have gone with Master Luke than stay here with you. I don't know what all this trouble is about, but I'm sure it must be your fault."

R2-D2 answered with a beeped expletive that only another droid would understand.

"You watch your language!" cried the offended C-3PO.

Facing the speeder dealer, Luke said, "All right, give it to me, I'll take it." The speeder dealer, an insectoid alien, had finally agreed to buy Luke's cherished landspeeder for two thousand credits.

Luke turned to Ben and showed him the credits. "Look at this," Luke said with dismay as they headed back for the droids. Luke had expected to get a few hundred more. He griped, "Ever since the XP-38 came out, they just aren't in demand."

"It will be enough," Ben told him.

As Ben and Luke proceeded through Mos Eisley's back alleys, they were followed by a Kubaz, an alien with a short, prehensile trunk for a nose. The Kubaz wore protective goggles and a dark cloak, and worked as an information dealer and spy for hire. One of his current clients was an Imperial stormtrooper squad leader.

The Kubaz didn't let Ben and Luke out of his sight.

✦

A short walk from the Mos Eisley cantina, Docking Bay 94 was a large circular pit that had been excavated from the sandy bedrock and reinforced with duracrete. It had an open roof, high surrounding walls, and was barely large enough to contain the YT-1300 Corellian freighter that rested on its floor. The freighter was Han Solo's ship, the *Millennium Falcon.*

Several figures moved around under the *Falcon*'s hull. Most of the figures carried blasters, but one didn't. He was a Hutt, a corpulent slug-like alien with a bulbous, wide-mouthed head and a tapering, muscular tail. He happened to be the most powerful crimelord in the Tatooine system, and all the other figures in the docking bay worked for him. Until very recently, he had also employed a hit man named Greedo. The gangster's name was Jabba.

"Solo," Jabba bellowed in Huttese at the *Falcon.* "Come out of there, Solo!"

"Right here, Jabba!" Han called from behind the Hutt.

Jabba twisted his bulky form to see Solo and Chewbacca enter the docking bay from the passage that led up to the street. Chewbacca was casually carrying his bowcaster.

Grinning at Jabba, Solo said, "I've been waiting for you."

"Have you now?" Jabba replied.

Han sauntered forward and said, "You didn't think I was gonna run, did you?"

"Han, my boy, you disappoint me," Jabba observed. "Why haven't you paid me? Why did you fry poor Greedo?"

"Look, Jabba, next time you want to talk to me, come see me yourself. Don't send one of these twerps." Han gestured at Jabba's blaster-wielding henchmen, including a man who wore a head-concealing helmet and antique body armour: a notoriously dangerous bounty hunter named Boba Fett.

"Han, I can't make exceptions." Jabba shrugged. "What if everyone who smuggled for me dropped their cargo at the first sign of an Imperial starship? It's not good for business."

"Look, Jabba, even I get boarded sometimes. You think I had a choice? I got a nice easy charter now. Pay you back, plus a little extra. I just need a little more time."

Jabba said, "Han, my boy, you're the best. So, for an extra twenty percent . . ."

"Fifteen, Jabba," Han said testily. "Don't push it."

"OK, fifteen percent," Jabba agreed. "But if you fail me again, I'll put a price on your head so big, you won't be able to go near a civilised system."

Turning to the *Falcon*'s landing ramp, Han added, "Jabba, you're a wonderful human being." Chewbacca followed Solo into the *Falcon*.

Jabba glared at his hired thugs and said, "Come on," then turned and slithered out of the docking bay.

Ben muttered, "If the ship's as fast as he's boasting, we ought to do well." He was walking alongside Luke through an alleyway that led to Docking Bay 94. They had just recovered C-3PO and R2-D2 from their hiding place, and the droids now followed in their tracks.

They rounded a corner and found Chewbacca standing in the docking bay entrance. He looked restless, and they wasted no time following him through the doorway.

Across from Docking Bay 94, on the other side of the alley, the Kubaz spy watched from the shadows. After the droids had passed through the entrance, the Kubaz lifted a comlink to his face and summoned the stormtroopers.

Ben, Luke and the droids followed Chewbacca down a flight of steps to the docking bay floor. When they arrived before the *Millennium Falcon*, they stopped and stared at the ship while Chewbacca headed up the ship's landing ramp.

Luke couldn't believe his eyes. The cockpit that projected out from the starboard side and the long forward mandibles made the *Falcon* recognisable as an old Corellian freighter, but the entire ship appeared to have been slapped together from used or rejected parts. To add further insult to the original design, a ridiculously oversized sensor dish was affixed to the top. The sight made Luke suddenly reconsider how he and Ben had invested their money.

Han was standing below the *Falcon*'s hull, checking the umbilicals' connection as he topped off the fuel tanks. Not caring whether Han could hear him, Luke commented, "What a piece of junk."

Han heard, but he'd heard worse and didn't care. "She'll make point five past lightspeed," he said, stepping away from the umbilicals. "She may not look like much, but she's got it where it counts, kid." With pride, he added, "I've made a lot of special modifications myself. But we're a little rushed, so if you'll just get on board, we'll get out of here."

The droids followed Ben and Luke to the *Falcon*'s landing ramp. As C-3PO passed Han, he said, "Hello, sir."

Han looked away and shook his head. He didn't care much for overly polite droids.

At the top of the landing ramp, Ben, Luke and the droids turned left through a passage tube. They passed a connecting passage tube that led to the cockpit, where Chewbacca was preparing the ship for lift-off, and arrived in the main hold. In a corner to the right, a three-passenger seat wrapped around a circular holographic game board. On the left, there was an engineering station with numerous scopes and controls, some of which appeared to have been secured with tape and glue. Most of the wall and ceiling panels were missing, leaving wires and machinery exposed.

Luke's initial reaction was that the *Falcon* looked even worse on the inside, and he didn't feel any better when he gave the engineering station a closer inspection. *These are Han's special modifications? I've never seen half of these components, and the ones I recognise aren't even compatible with one another. I'll be amazed if this thing even gets off the ground!*

The stormtrooper squad found the Kubaz spy waiting for them outside Docking Bay 94. The squad leader stopped in front of the Kubaz and said, "Which way?"

The spy pointed to the docking bay entrance.

"All right, men," commanded the squad leader. "Load your weapons!" Then the seven stormtroopers descended the steps that led to the docking bay floor.

Han was under the *Falcon*, disconnecting the umbilicals, when he saw the stormtrooper squad charge into the docking bay. One of the troopers shouted, "Stop that ship!"

Three troopers immediately opened fire. Han

snapped his blaster from his holster and shot back at the troopers.

"Blast 'em!" ordered the stormtrooper squad leader.

Han aimed high to hit the duracrete ceiling above the troopers' heads. His fired bolts struck the ceiling with explosive force, sending large chunks of duracrete down upon the astonished soldiers. Han didn't stop firing until he was halfway up the landing ramp.

"Chewie, get us out of here!" Han shouted as he sealed the ramp's access hatch and bolted to the cockpit. The engines kicked on and the entire ship trembled in response.

In the main hold, R2-D2 used his magnetic grips to secure himself to the deck while Luke, Ben and C-3PO belted into the seat that wrapped around the game table. C-3PO cried, "Oh, my, I'd forgotten how much I hate space travel."

The stormtroopers continued firing as the *Falcon* – without the benefit of lift-off clearance from the spaceport authority – thrust up through the open roof of the docking bay. On a nearby street in Mos Eisley, another stormtrooper squad heard the roar of the *Falcon*'s engines. The troopers turned in time to glimpse the fleeing ship's sub-light drive exhaust blaze with intense light. The ship ascended rapidly into the pale blue sky.

As Chewbacca guided the *Falcon* up through

Tatooine's atmosphere and into space, he pointed to the radar scope and barked at Han. Han glanced at the scope and said, "Looks like an Imperial cruiser. Our passengers must be hotter than I thought. Try and hold them off. Angle the deflector shield while I make the calculations for the jump to lightspeed."

Han rose from his seat to flip a series of control switches. He was still making his calculations when he jumped back into his seat. He saw two larger blips appear on the radar screen. According to the readout, each blip was an Imperial Star Destroyer.

"Stay sharp!" Han told Chewbacca. "There are two more coming in; they're going to try to cut us off."

Just then, Luke and Ben rushed into the cockpit and clung to the two seats behind Han and Chewbacca. They had heard Han's announcement regarding the incoming ships, and saw a clear field of stars beyond the cockpit window. Luke asked, "Why don't you outrun them? I thought you said this thing was fast."

Han tossed a glare at Luke and said, "Watch your mouth, kid, or you're going to find yourself floating home. We'll be safe enough once we make the jump to hyperspace. Besides, I know a few manoeuvres. We'll lose them!"

The Star Destroyers fired at the *Falcon* and a bright flash exploded outside the cockpit. Another volley of laserfire pounded the *Falcon*'s deflector shields, causing the ship to rock violently. Han grinned as he tightened his grip on the controls and said, "Here's where the fun begins!"

Ben said, "How long before you can make the jump to lightspeed?"

Han told him, "It'll take a few moments to get the coordinates from the nav computer." The *Falcon* shook again as its shields took another hit.

"Are you kidding?" Luke couldn't believe it. "At the rate they're gaining . . ."

"Travelling through hyperspace isn't like dusting crops, boy!" Han snapped. "Without precise calculations we could fly right through a star or bounce too close to a supernova and that'd end your trip real quick, wouldn't it?"

A red warning light activated in front of Chewbacca. Luke extended his arm to point at the light and asked, "What's that flashing?"

"We're losing our deflector shield," Han said, slapping Luke's hand away. "Go strap yourselves in. I'm going to make the jump to lightspeed."

Luke and Ben left the cockpit and returned to the hold. Han reached for the hyperdrive controls and threw the ignition switch.

Suddenly, the field of distant stars was transformed into long streaks of light that radiated from infinity and appeared to sweep over the ship. The *Falcon* had entered hyperspace, a dimension of space time that allowed faster-than-light travel across the galaxy. And because it was impossible to follow a ship through hyperspace, the *Falcon* had effectively escaped the two Star Destroyers.

But as fast as the *Millennium Falcon* could travel, the little astromech droid would never be delivered to the planet Alderaan.

CHAPTER 8

"**WE'VE** entered the Alderaan system," Admiral Motti announced to Grand Moff Tarkin. They were in the control room on the Death Star. Tarkin stood before a wide viewscreen that displayed a small green planet. At the sound of approaching footsteps, Tarkin and Mott turned to face an adjoining corridor.

Two black-uniformed Imperial soldiers led Princess Leia through the corridor and into the control room. A pair of binders secured Leia's wrists in front of her. Behind her, Darth Vader followed like a malevolent shadow.

"Governor Tarkin," Leia said. "I should have expected to find you holding Vader's leash. I recognised your foul stench when I was brought on board."

Tarkin smiled. "Charming to the last." He reached out to touch Leia's chin and said, "You don't know how hard I found it signing the order to terminate your life!"

Leia jerked her head away from Tarkin's hand and

said, "I'm surprised you had the courage to take the responsibility yourself!"

Tarkin said, "Princess Leia, before your execution I would like you to be my guest at a ceremony that will make this battle station operational. No star system will dare oppose the Emperor now."

If Leia was even slightly frightened, she didn't show it. She said, "The more you tighten your grip, Tarkin, the more star systems will slip through your fingers."

"Not after we demonstrate the power of this station," Tarkin informed her with confidence. "In a way, you have determined the choice of the planet that will be destroyed first. Since you are reluctant to provide us with the location of the rebel base, I have chosen to test this station's destructive power . . . on your home planet of Alderaan." He gestured to the viewport.

At the sight of her homeworld, Leia's confident expression became suddenly fearful. "*No!*" she protested. "Alderaan is peaceful. We have no weapons. You can't possibly –"

"You would prefer another target?" Tarkin interrupted. "A military target? Then name the system!"

Leia thought, *He's insane. He's completely insane.*

Tarkin continued, "I grow tired of asking this. So it'll be the last time." He advanced toward Leia, forcing her to step backward into Vader. "Where is the rebel base?"

Leia trembled against Vader. *There are billions of*

people on Alderaan! What can I do to save them? She gazed past Tarkin's shoulder to look again at Alderaan on the viewport. "Dantooine," she said, then lowered her head. "They're on Dantooine."

"There," Tarkin said with satisfaction. "You see, Lord Vader, she can be reasonable." Then Tarkin turned to Admiral Motti and said, "Continue with the operation. You may fire when ready."

"What?" Leia gasped as Motti stepped away to a control console.

"You're far too trusting," Tarkin said. "Dantooine is too remote to make an effective demonstration. But don't worry. We will deal with your rebel friends soon enough."

Leia stepped toward Tarkin and cried, "No!" Then she felt Vader's cold, tight grip on her arm, pulling her back to him and away from Tarkin.

An intercom voice announced, "Commence primary ignition."

Leia heard the sounds of generators powering up, but kept her stunned eyes on the viewscreen. Even from space, Alderaan was lushly beautiful, its snow-topped mountains and grassy plains making the world resemble an emerald amidst the stars. She knew its geography so well that she could – from her perspective on the Death Star – pinpoint the capital, where she'd grown up . . . where her father still lived. After the battle of Scarif, in which the plans for the Death Star had been stolen, Bail Organa had returned home to tell his people that war was coming . . . but his warning would come too late.

Father, I'm so sorry.

Leia couldn't believe that all her friends and loved ones, every person and every cherished place was about to be annihilated. And all because no one had opposed the Empire before the construction of the Death Star. Even as she saw the space station's green laser beam streak out at her homeworld, Leia prayed for the Death Star to fail.

But it didn't. And in one explosive instant, Alderaan was gone.

Luke was in the *Millennium Falcon*'s hold, testing his lightsaber against a small, hovering remote target globe when Ben suddenly turned away and sat down near the engineering station. Seeing that Ben seemed almost faint, Luke switched off the lightsaber and asked, "Are you all right? What's wrong?"

"I felt a great disturbance in the Force," Ben said. "As if millions of voices suddenly cried out in terror and were suddenly silenced. I fear something terrible has happened." He rubbed his eyes. Not wanting to worry Luke, he added, "You'd better get on with your exercises."

Luke nodded and turned away from Ben. He glanced

to the corner seat, where Chewbacca and R2-D2 were competing at the holographic game table, with C-3PO serving as referee.

Luke stepped back to the centre of the hold, activated his lightsaber, and returned his attention to the hovering remote. Ben had rightly assumed that Han kept a remote on board for quick-draw target practice, and had programmed the device to fire harmless sting bursts for Luke to deflect with his lightsaber. Luke kept his eyes on the remote and batted at two fired bursts as Han Solo entered the hold.

"Well, you can forget your troubles with those Imperial ships," Han said as he took a seat at the engineering station. "I told you I'd outrun 'em."

Han looked around the hold. Luke continued swinging his lightsaber at sting bursts from the remote. Chewie and the droids continued playing their game. Ben looked like he had a headache.

Han grumbled, "Don't everybody thank me at once. Anyway, we should be at Alderaan at about oh two hundred hours."

Han looked back to the action at the game table. From the holographic creatures that appeared to stand upon the table's gold-and-green chequer-patterned surface, Han could see Chewbacca and R2-D2 were playing dejarik. R2-D2 moved a multi-legged blue houjix. Chewbacca countered by sending his Kintan strider – a yellow-skinned biped that carried a club - two steps across the table. Han thought Chewie looked pleased with himself.

C-3PO said, "Now be careful, Artoo."

R2-D2 moved his Mantellian savrip - a hunched-over creature with a snake-like neck and long, powerful arms - over to Chewbacca's just-moved Kintan strider. The savrip seized the Kintan strider, hoisted it up, then smashed it down upon the game table.

Chewbacca growled angrily at R2-D2.

"He made a fair move," C-3PO observed in response. "Screaming about it can't help you."

Han said, "Let him have it. It's not wise to upset a Wookiee."

Turning to face Han, C-3PO said indignantly, "But sir, nobody worries about upsetting a droid."

Han grinned. "That's because a droid don't pull people's arms out of their sockets when they lose. Wookiees are known to do that."

C-3PO looked at Chewbacca, who raised his arms and cupped his hands behind his head, flexing his hirsute muscles. C-3PO turned back to Han and said, "I see your point, sir." Leaning over to R2-D2, C-3PO advised, "I suggest a new strategy, Artoo-Detoo. Let the Wookiee win."

R2-D2 answered with a surprised beep. Chewbacca chortled happily.

When Ben felt somewhat recovered, he resumed watching Luke's practice with the remote. Luke's eyes followed the remote with intense concentration, but his movements were stiff, not relaxed. Ben said, "Remember, a Jedi can feel the Force flowing through him."

Luke said, "You mean it controls your actions?"

"Partially," Ben said. "But it also obeys your commands."

The remote hovered in a wide arc around Luke, then made a lightning-swift lunge and emitted a laser beam. At the engineering station, Han looked up just in time to see the beam strike Luke's leg.

Han laughed. "Hokey religions and ancient weapons are no match for a good blaster at your side, kid."

Luke deactivated his lightsaber and glared at Han. "You don't believe in the Force, do you?"

Han shook his head. "Kid, I've flown from one side of this galaxy to the other. I've seen a lot of strange stuff, but I've never seen anything to make me believe there's one all-powerful force controlling everything. There's no mystical energy field that controls my destiny."

Ben smiled quietly at Han's comment.

Han continued, "It's all a lot of simple tricks and nonsense."

Ben rose from his seat. "I suggest you try it again, Luke," he said, picking up a blast shield helmet from the engineering station. He placed the helmet over Luke's head and lowered the shield so it covered his eyes. "This time, let go of your conscious self and act on instinct."

Luke laughed. "With the blast shield down I can't even see. How am I supposed to fight?"

"Your eyes can deceive you," Ben said. "Don't trust them."

Luke activated his lightsaber and assumed a ready stance. The remote hovered up and moved around his body. *Don't trust my eyes? I can barely hear the remote! I think it's on my left . . . No, it's . . .*

Luke was stung by another laserbolt.

. . . it's not where I thought it was.

Ben said, "Stretch out with your feelings."

Keeping the helmet on and his blade activated, Luke resumed a ready stance. He stopped thinking about the remote, just stopped thinking and relaxed, and . . . somehow, he sensed the remote's proximity. Stranger still, he seemed able to anticipate its movement through the air.

The remote fired three bursts in quick succession. Despite his blocked vision, Luke moved fast with his lightsaber and deftly parried each shot.

He switched off his lightsaber and pulled off the helmet. Ben sounded glad when he said, "You see, you can do it."

Han said, "I call it luck."

Ben replied, "In my experience, there is no such thing as luck."

Han would not be convinced. "Look, good against remotes is one thing. Good against the living? That's something else." A light flashed on a scope at the engineering station. "Looks like we're coming up on Alderaan."

Han rose from his seat and headed out of the hold to the cockpit. Chewbacca followed him.

Facing Ben, Luke said, "You know, I did feel something. I could almost see the remote."

"That's good," Ben told his new pupil, placing a hand on Luke's shoulder. "You have taken your first step into a larger world."

On the Death Star, Major Cass, a white-haired adjutant to Grand Moff Tarkin, entered the conference room. He found Darth Vader standing at one end of the round table at the room's centre, with Tarkin seated across from him at the other end. Tarkin looked up from the table's data screen and said, "Yes."

"Our scout ships have reached Dantooine," Cass reported. "They found the remains of a rebel base, but they estimate that it has been deserted for some time. They are now conducting an extensive search of the surrounding systems." Having delivered his report, Cass turned and exited the room.

"She lied!" Tarkin was outraged, rising from the table to approach Vader. "She lied to us!"

Indeed, that was just what Princess Leia had done. Vader said, "I told you she would never consciously betray the Rebellion."

Tarkin scowled at Vader. "Terminate her . . . immediately!"

Blue and white shimmers of energy flowed past the *Falcon* as it neared the end of its trip through hyperspace. Han and Chewbacca were seated in the cockpit. Han said, "Stand by, Chewie. Here we go." He threw a lever to kill the hyperdrive, then added, "Cut in the sub-light engines."

The *Falcon* decelerated and dropped into realspace. The energy shimmers that had been visible outside the cockpit window were replaced by a field of distant stars, along with an immediate barrage of unexpected debris.

"What the . . . ?" Han said as floating chunks of matter hammered at the *Falcon*'s particle shields. "Aw, we've come out of hyperspace into a meteor shower. Some kind of asteroid collision. It's not on any of the charts."

Responding to the hammering racket outside the ship, Luke and Ben entered the cockpit. Luke stood behind Chewbacca's seat and asked, "What's going on?"

Han explained, "Our position is correct, except . . . no Alderaan!"

"What do you mean?" Luke didn't understand. "Where is it?"

"That's what I'm trying to tell you, kid. It ain't there. It's been totally blown away."

"What? How?"

From behind Chewbacca, Ben said, "Destroyed . . . by the Empire!"

Han was doubtful. "The entire starfleet couldn't destroy the whole planet. It'd take a thousand ships with more firepower than I've –" An alarm sounded and Han glanced at a sensor scope. "There's another ship coming in."

Luke said, "Maybe *they* know what happened."

Without yet seeing the other ship, Ben said, "It's an Imperial fighter."

As if in response to Ben's words, a huge explosion burst outside the cockpit window, then an Imperial TIE fighter streaked past the *Falcon*. The Twin Ion Engine ship was immediately recognisable by its two hexagonal solar array wings on either side of a small, spherical command pod.

Luke said, "It followed us!"

"No," Ben observed. "It's a short-range fighter."

Han said, "There aren't any bases around here. Where did it come from?"

"It sure is leaving in a big hurry," Luke noticed as the TIE fighter sped away from the *Falcon*. "If they identify us, we're in big trouble."

"Not if I can help it," Han said, steering after the TIE fighter and away from the planetary debris. "Chewie - jam its transmissions."

"It'd be as well to let it go," Ben said. "It's too far out of range."

"Not for long . . ." Han increased power to the sublight engines.

Ben said, "A fighter that size couldn't get this deep into space on its own."

Luke added, "Then he must have gotten lost, been part of a convoy or something . . ."

Han said, "Well, he ain't going to be around long enough to tell anybody about us."

"Look at him," Luke said. "He's heading for that small moon."

Han saw the moon too, and said, "I think I can get him before he gets there . . . he's almost in range."

Ben went rigid in his seat. "That's no moon! It's a space station."

Han replied, "It's too big to be a space station." But even before he'd finished, Han sounded doubtful of his own words. Like the others in the cockpit, he could now make out surface details on the object in view, and the details had an unnatural symmetry.

Luke said, "I have a very bad feeling about this."

"Turn the ship around!" Ben insisted.

"Yeah," Han agreed. "I think you're right. Full reverse! Chewie, lock in the auxiliary power."

Chewbacca did as instructed, but the *Falcon* began to shake violently and continued to travel after the TIE fighter and toward the object, which was now clearly visible as a space station.

"Chewie, lock in the auxiliary power!" Han repeated, shouting over the noise of the shaking ship.

Hanging on to his seat, Luke said, "Why are we still moving toward it?"

"We're caught in a tractor beam!" Han explained. "It's pulling us in."

Tractor beams were modified force fields that immobilised objects and moved them within the range of the beam projector. Hangar bays and spaceports generally used tractor beams to help guide ships to safe landings, but the beams could also be used to capture enemy ships. And in this case, it seemed the *Falcon* was someone's enemy.

The *Falcon*'s engines and deflector shields were ineffective for escape. By attempting to send the ship into full reverse, Han was only producing friction within the tractor beam, hence the shaking. The tractor beam also immobilised the *Falcon*'s weapons, rendering them useless; any attempt to fire at the space station would likely cause the weapons themselves to blow up.

Luke said, “There’s gotta be something you can do!”

“There’s nothin’ I can do about it, kid,” Han said. “I’m in full power. I’m going to have to shut down. But they’re not going to get me without a fight!” Han powered down the engines and the *Falcon* stopped shaking.

“You can’t win,” Ben told Han. “But there are alternatives to fighting.”

Luke couldn’t imagine what Ben had in mind, but he hoped the plan didn’t require much time. At the speed the *Falcon* was travelling toward the space station, time was something they just didn’t have.

CHAPTER 9

THE tractor beam pulled the *Millennium Falcon* straight toward the Death Star's equatorial trench. Along the trench's walls, laser turret cannons tracked the captured ship as it was drawn toward a docking bay. Because of the space station's enormous size, the docking bay – from a distance – resembled little more than a small slot that neighboured other slots within the trench. The bay was without visible doors and its interior appeared to be exposed to the vacuum of space, an illusion created by a transparent magnetic field that shielded and contained the docking bay's pressurised atmosphere.

Over an Imperial intercom, a voice announced, "Clear Bay Three-twenty-seven. We are opening the magnetic field." The field opened, allowing the *Falcon* to pass through the slot-like doorway and hover into Docking Bay 327, a wide hangar with a gleaming black deck. After the tractor beam safely deposited the

Falcon on the deck beside a deep elevator well, the Imperial soldiers prepared to enter the docking bay.

"To your stations!" a black-uniformed Imperial officer commanded a group of stormtroopers in a chamber that adjoined the hangar. The officer turned to another officer and said, "Come with me."

The stormtroopers quickly took up position around the captured Corellian freighter. An officer ordered, "Close all outboard shields! Close all outboard shields!"

Grand Moff Tarkin and Darth Vader were still in the conference room when an intercom buzzed. Tarkin pushed a button and said, "Yes."

From the intercom, an Imperial officer announced, "We've captured a freighter entering the remains of the Alderaan system. Its markings match those of a ship that blasted its way out of Mos Eisley."

Vader said, "They must be trying to return the stolen plans to the princess. She may yet be of some use to us."

After Vader was informed of the captured freighter's location, he swept out of the conference room and headed for Docking Bay 327.

As Darth Vader entered the hangar that contained the *Millennium Falcon*, a voice over the intercom said, "Unlock one, five, seven and nine. Release charges." Vader walked past the elevator well and the stormtroopers who stood guard on the hangar floor, and approached the *Falcon*'s lowered landing ramp.

A grey-uniformed Imperial captain and a pair of stormtroopers stepped down the landing ramp. The captain stopped in front of Vader and said, "There's no one on board, sir. According to the log, the crew abandoned ship right after take-off. It must be a decoy, sir. Several of the escape pods have been jettisoned."

Vader said, "Did you find any droids?"

"No, sir," the captain reported. "If there were any on board, they must also have been jettisoned."

"Send a scanning crew aboard," Vader ordered. "I want every part of the ship checked."

"Yes, sir."

Vader looked up at the ship's hull and said, "I sense something . . . a presence I've not felt since . . ."

Then it hit him.

Obi-Wan Kenobi.

He's alive.

Trusting the ship would be thoroughly checked, Vader turned fast and headed for the conference room.

The Imperial captain turned to a stormtrooper and said, "Get me a scanning crew in here on the double. I want every part of this ship checked!"

While waiting for the scanning crew to arrive, two blaster-wielding stormtroopers walked in opposite directions through the *Falcon's* passage tubes to reconnoitre the holds and cargo compartments. When the two stormtroopers reunited at the top of the landing ramp, they exited the ship satisfied that no passengers remained on board.

But inside the *Falcon*, a floor panel popped up from the passage tube; Luke and Han emerged from their hiding place: a large compartment under the floor. Han had his blaster pistol out and ready.

Luke said, "Boy, it's lucky you had these compartments."

"I use them for smuggling," Han explained. "I never thought I'd be smuggling *myself* in them."

Near Han and Luke another floor panel slid back to reveal Ben hiding in the same compartment. Ben moved slowly, careful not to bump into the two droids who were squeezed in beneath him.

"This is ridiculous," Han said. "Even if I could take off, I'd never get past the tractor beam."

"Leave that to me!" Ben said.

"Damn fool," Han muttered as he lifted himself up to sit at the edge of the compartment. "I *knew* you were going to say that!"

Ben said dryly, "Who's the more foolish – the fool or the fool who follows him?"

Chewbacca raised his furry head up between

Luke and Han. The Wookiee moaned with displeasure at the way he'd had to cram his large body into the compartment. Sympathetic, Han reached down and patted Chewbacca's head.

The scanning crew consisted of two grey-uniformed men with a large box of equipment. When they arrived in the hangar, two stormtrooper squads were on guard outside the *Falcon*. A stormtrooper squad leader approached the scanning crew and said, "The ship's all yours. If the scanners pick up anything, report it immediately." Then the squad leader turned to the other troopers and said, "All right, let's go."

Two remained stationed at the bottom of the *Falcon*'s landing ramp, while the other troopers filed out of the hangar. A moment after the scanning crew carried their equipment box up the ramp, there was a loud crashing sound from inside the ship. Both stormtroopers assumed the scanning crew had dropped the large box.

"Hey down there!" a man's voice called from inside the *Falcon*. "Could you give us a hand with this?"

The two stormtroopers glanced at each other, then marched up the landing ramp. They had no idea that the scanning crew had already been knocked out, and that it had been the *Falcon*'s captain who'd just summoned them into the ship.

Han fired his blaster pistol twice. The stormtroopers never knew what hit them.

In the command office that overlooked Docking Bay 327, a black-uniformed gantry officer noticed the two stormtrooper guards were missing from their stations at the captured ship's landing ramp. He stepped to a comm console, flipped on the comlink, and said, "TK-four-two-one. Why aren't you at your post? TK-four-two-one, do you copy?"

When no answer came, the officer stepped away from the console to a window and peered through it, looking down at the freighter on the hangar deck. A single stormtrooper stepped down the landing ramp, then stopped and looked up in the direction of the command-office window. The stormtrooper tapped at the side of his helmet.

The gantry officer turned to his aide, who was seated before a wide control console, and said, "Take over. We've got a bad transmitter. I'll see what I can do."

The gantry officer walked to a closed doorway. He pressed a button, and the door slid up into the ceiling. The officer had expected to see an empty corridor leading to a lift-tube that would carry him down to the hangar. To his astonishment, a hulking Wookiee filled the doorway with a stormtrooper at his side.

The Wookiee roared and lashed out at the officer,

launching him across the room to smash into a row of barrel-shaped containers. The officer's aide spun in his seat and reached for his blaster, but the stormtrooper beside the Wookiee aimed his own blaster rifle at the aide and fired first. The energy charge slammed into the aide's chest, and he collapsed to the office floor.

The stormtrooper was Han in disguise. He pulled off his helmet as he and Chewbacca led Ben and the droids into the command office.

Luke, also disguised as a stormtrooper, had left the hangar deck quickly and now came trotting up the corridor behind them. He had a hard time moving in his appropriated armour because he was slightly shorter than the average trooper. Entering the command office, he shut the door behind him, then pulled off his white helmet and glared at Han. "You know, between his howling and your blasting everything in sight, it's a wonder the whole station doesn't know we're here."

"Bring them on!" Han said. "I prefer a straight fight to all this sneaking around."

The droids had moved over beside the aide's vacated seat at the control console. Turning to Luke, C-3PO said, "We found the computer outlet, sir."

Ben said, "Plug in. He should be able to interpret the entire Imperial network."

R2-D2 extended a manipulator arm into the computer outlet and beeped to C-3PO, who translated,

"He says he's found the main controls to the power beam that's holding the ship here. He'll try to make the precise location appear on the monitor."

Everyone looked to a small viewscreen that displayed a series of green-coloured readouts. R2-D2 beeped again. C-3PO said, "The tractor beam is coupled to the main reactor in seven locations. A power loss at one of the terminals will allow the ship to leave."

Ben studied the schematics for the power generator terminal that was displayed on the viewscreen, then turned to Luke and Han and said, "I don't think you boys can help. I must go alone."

"Whatever you say," Han replied as Ben headed for the door. "I've done more than I bargained for on this trip already."

Luke stopped Ben at the door and said, "I want to go with you."

"Be patient, Luke," Ben said. "Stay and watch over the droids."

Luke gestured at Han and said, "But he can –"

Ben interrupted, "They must be delivered safely or other star systems will suffer the same fate as Alderaan. Your destiny lies along a different path from mine." Ben pressed a button on the doorway, sending the door up into the ceiling. Facing Luke, he added, "The Force will be with you . . . always!"

Ben left the command office and moved down the

corridor. Luke watched Ben's departing form, then reluctantly pressed the button and sealed the doorway.

Chewbacca tilted back his head and barked.

"Boy, you said it, Chewie," Han agreed. Looking to Luke, he added, "Where did you dig up that old fossil?"

"Ben is a great man," Luke said defensively.

"Yeah," Han said, "great at getting us into trouble."

"I didn't hear you give any ideas . . ."

"Well, anything's better than just hanging around waiting for them to pick us up."

"Who do you think –"

The argument was interrupted by R2-D2, who was still plugged into the computer socket and suddenly began to whistle and beep agitatedly.

Luke turned to the droids and asked, "What is it?"

"I'm afraid I'm not quite sure, sir," C-3PO said. "He says 'I found her' and keeps repeating 'She's here.'"

Dumbfounded, Luke stepped over to the droids. "Well, who . . . who has he found?"

"Princess Leia."

"The princess?" Luke said, his eyes wide with surprise. "She's here?"

"Princess?" Han echoed from beside Chewbacca on the other side of the command office. Neither of them had heard anything about a princess.

Luke asked, "Where . . . where is she?"

"Princess?" Han repeated. "What's going on?"

R2-D2 made whirring and clicking sounds as he scanned the computer, then beeped to C-3PO.

C-3PO translated, "Level five. Detention block AA-twenty-three."

But R2-D2 wasn't finished, and emitted more beeps.

The protocol droid's voice filled with concern as he reported, "I'm afraid she's scheduled to be terminated."

"Oh, no!" Luke exclaimed. "We've got to do something."

"What are you talking about?" Han asked.

"The droids belonged to her," Luke replied. "She's the one in the message. We've got to help her."

Han and Chewbacca had never heard anything about a message either. Han warned, "No, look, don't get any funny ideas. The old man wants us to wait right here."

"But he didn't know she was here," Luke pointed out. Turning back to R2-D2, he said, "Look, will you just find a way back into that detention block?"

Han sat down and put his feet up on the console. "I'm not going anywhere," he said.

"They're going to execute her," Luke said. "Look, a few minutes ago you said you didn't want to just wait here to be captured. Now all you want to do is stay."

"Marching into the detention area is not what I had in mind." Han wasn't budging from his seat.

"But they're going to kill her!"

"Better her than me."

I can't do this alone, Luke thought. *I've got to think of something – anything – that will convince Han to help.* Then he had it. Leaning down beside Han, he said, "She's rich."

That got Han's attention. He turned his head slightly. "Rich?"

Luke nodded. "Rich, powerful! Listen, if you were to rescue her, the reward would be . . ."

"What?"

"Well, more wealth than you can imagine."

"I don't know," Han said, "I can imagine quite a bit!"

"You'll get it!"

"I'd better!"

"You will."

"All right, kid," Han said, rising from his seat. "But you'd better be right about this!"

"All right," Luke responded. *Now we're getting somewhere!*

"What's your plan?"

Plan? Luke wondered how far he and Han might get in their stormtrooper disguises, then looked at Chewbacca and had an idea. "Uh . . . Threepio, hand me those binders there, will you?"

The protocol droid picked up a pair of metal binders that happened to be lying on the control console and gave them to Luke.

"OK." Luke held out the binders as he approached Chewbacca. "Now, I'm going to put these on you."

Chewbacca roared sharply and Luke stumbled backward. Luke handed the binders to Han and stammered, "OK – Han, you . . . you put those on."

"Don't worry, Chewie," Han soothed as he carried the binders to the Wookiee. "I think I know what he has in mind."

Han placed the binders over the Wookiee's thick wrists but didn't lock them. Luke handed a small comlink transmitter over to C-3PO. Then Luke and Han picked up their helmets and headed for the door with Chewbacca.

"Er, Master Luke, sir!" C-3PO said nervously. "Pardon me for asking . . . but . . . what should Artoo-Detoo and I do if we're discovered here?"

"Lock the door!" Luke said.

"And hope they don't have blasters," Han added.

"That isn't very reassuring," C-3PO said, clapping his hand down upon R2-D2's domed head as the two men and the Wookiee left the room.

CHAPTER 10

IN their stormtrooper disguises, Luke and Han escorted Chewbacca through a Death Star corridor. There had been no getting around the fact that Luke looked suspiciously small for a stormtrooper, and the effect was worse when he stood next to Han. They'd agreed that Han would walk slightly ahead and to the right of Chewbacca while Luke would stay close to Chewbacca's left side. It was their hope that any casual passer-by would notice the towering Wookiee, not the height of the stormtrooper beside him. This arrangement was also some relief to Luke, who was barely able to peer through the lenses of his oversized helmet. As he gripped the Wookiee's elbow, it may have looked like he was guiding a bound captive through the corridor, but in fact, Chewbacca was guiding him.

They were heading for a lift-tube that would carry them to level five when Chewbacca saw a small MSE-6 droid move toward them. The box-shaped droid travelled on four wheels and was used to deliver orders and documents. Chewbacca roared at the droid for no other reason than he felt like it. The droid shrieked and raced away from him. Chewbacca looked at the stormtrooper to his left - Luke - and barked with amusement.

They proceeded to a row of lift-tubes, passing troops, bureaucrats and droids who were also walking through the corridor. As expected, only Chewbacca drew any stares.

As they waited for the lift-tube doors to open, Luke muttered, "I can't see a thing in this helmet."

The lift opened and they stepped in. A grey-uniformed bureaucrat attempted to follow them, but Han held up a cautioning hand to discourage him. The bureaucrat moved on to another lift.

The lift-tube doors closed. Han pressed the button for level five and said, "This is not going to work."

"Why didn't you say so before?" Luke said.

"I *did* say so before!"

They'd been expecting the door to open in front of them, and were surprised when they heard it open from behind. They turned and stepped into detention block AA-23.

An Imperial lieutenant stood behind a semicircular control station of the detention security area. Behind him, two black-uniformed soldiers stood against a wall, and a short flight of steps led up to a cell corridor, where a third soldier appeared to be inspecting cell doors.

The lieutenant at the control station sneered at the sight of Chewbacca and said, "Where are you taking this . . . thing?"

"Prisoner transfer from Cell Block one-one-three-eight," Luke said.

"I wasn't notified," the lieutenant replied. "I'll have to clear it." He signalled to the two nearby guards. Both guards drew their blasters, then one approached Chewbacca.

Chewbacca roared and lashed out with one mighty hand, smashing the guard with enough strength to launch him off his feet. Then came total chaos.

Han shouted, "Look out! He's loose!" and tossed his blaster rifle to Chewbacca.

Luke shouted, "He's going to pull us apart!" as he fired at the startled guards. Chewbacca started shooting at the security-camera eyes and laser-gate controls. Laserbolts pinged and exploded all over the room.

Han shouted, "Go get him!" and grabbed a blaster from a fallen guard. The lieutenant finally realised that Han and Luke weren't real stormtroopers and reached for his own blaster. Han disabled him. Then he, Luke and Chewbacca kept blasting until every security sensor was a shattered mess.

The lieutenant had collapsed on top of his control

station, where an alarm was beeping wildly. While Chewbacca clutched his Imperial blaster rifle and watched the lift-tube doors, Luke hurried into the control station and pulled the lieutenant's body aside.

Han ran up beside Luke and said, "We've got to find out which cell this princess of yours is in." He scanned a data screen. "Here it is . . . twenty-one-eighty-seven. You go and get her. I'll hold them here."

Luke ran up the steps and entered the detention corridor. Han removed his stormtrooper helmet and placed it beside his blaster rifle on the console. He switched off the beeping alarm, flicked on the comlink system and said in a calm tone, "Everything's under control. Situation normal."

Over the intercom, a voice asked, "What happened?"

"Uh . . . had a slight weapons malfunction," Han said, trying to sound official. "But, uh, everything's perfectly all right now. We're fine. We're all fine here now, thank you. How are you?" Han winced at the lameness of his own words.

"We're sending a squad up," came the voice from the intercom.

"Uh, uh, negative, negative," Han said. "We have a reactor leak here now. Give us a few minutes to lock it down. Large leak . . . very dangerous."

"Who is this?" came the intercom voice. "What's your operating number?"

Han briefly considered answering, then picked up the blaster rifle, aimed it at the comlink system, and fired at point-blank range, shattering the system. "Boring conversation anyway," he muttered, then turned to look down the detention corridor and shouted, "Luke! We're going to have company!"

Luke heard, and ran faster, past the recessed doorways that lined the corridor. When he found cell 2187, he slapped a button on the wall and the cell door slid up.

And then he saw her.

Princess Leia was sleeping on the bare metal slab that served as a bed. She appeared to be wearing the same white gown that she'd worn when she'd made the holographic recording. Luke stepped down into the cell, thinking, *She's so beautiful.*

Leia opened her eyes and lifted her head. She had an uncomprehending look on her face as she said, "Aren't you a little short for a stormtrooper?"

"Huh?" Luke replied. "Oh . . . the uniform." He reached up to pull off the helmet. Shaking his hair free, he said, "I'm Luke Skywalker. I'm here to rescue you."

Leia remained on the slab and said, "You're who?"

"I'm here to rescue you. I've got your Artoo unit. I'm here with Ben Kenobi."

"Ben Kenobi!" Leia cried, jumping up. "Where is he?"

Luke said, "Come on!"

Leia ran past Luke and through the cell's open doorway, and he followed her out.

Tarkin sat at the far end of the round table in the conference room. Darth Vader stood at the other end and said, "He is here."

"Obi-Wan Kenobi!" Tarkin said. "What makes you think so?"

"A tremor in the Force. The last time I felt it was in the presence of my old Master."

Doubtful, Tarkin said, "Surely he must be dead by now."

"Don't underestimate the Force," Vader replied.

"The Jedi are extinct; their fire has gone out of the universe. You, my friend, are all that's left of their religion." A signal chimed from the comlink at the console in front of Tarkin's seat. Tarkin pressed a button on the console and said, "Yes."

On the intercom, a voice said, "We have an emergency alert in detention block AA-twenty-three."

"The princess!" Tarkin said. "Put all sections on alert!"

"Obi-Wan *is* here," Vader stated. "The Force is with him."

"If you're right, he must not be allowed to escape."

"Escape is not in his plan." Before turning for the door, Vader said knowingly, "I must face him alone."

+

Han and Chewbacca were still in the detention security area when they heard an ominous buzzing sound from the lift-tube doors. The Wookiee growled at the noise. Han shouted, "Get behind me! Get behind me!"

Chewbacca jumped away from the lift-tubes as an explosion ripped a large hole through one door. The hole's edges were still smouldering as the first stormtrooper stepped through. Han aimed and fired. The trooper fell, and another trooper pushed his way through the hole, followed by another.

Han and Chewbacca ran for the detention corridor. Behind them, one stormtrooper stopped the others and said, "Off to your left. They went down in the cell bay." The stormtroopers fired their blasters down the length of the detention corridor.

Inside the corridor, laserbolts whizzed past Luke and Leia. Because the cell doorways were recessed, the surrounding metal frames served as shallow protective alcoves. As Luke and Leia instinctively ducked against a door to avoid being hit, Han and Chewbacca came pounding up the corridor and threw themselves into neighbouring doorways. Glancing back down the corridor to the security area, Han shouted, "Can't get out that way."

"Looks like you managed to cut off our only escape route," Leia said angrily.

"Maybe you'd like it back in your cell, Your Highness," Han replied.

Luke remembered C-3PO and R2-D2 were still back at the command office that overlooked Docking Bay 327. Thinking the droids might be useful, Luke reached for his comlink and said into it, "See-Threepio! See-Threepio!"

From the comlink, the droid replied, "Yes, sir?"

Luke said, "Are there any other ways out of the cell bay? We've been cut off!" More laserbolts zinged through the corridor. Luke shouted into his comlink, "What was that? I didn't copy!"

"I said, all systems have been alerted to your presence, sir," C-3PO answered. "The main entrance seems to be the only way in or out; all other information on your level is restricted."

Just then, the droid heard someone banging on the command office's door. From the other side of it, a stormtrooper demanded, "Open up in there! Open up in there!"

"Oh, no!" C-3PO cried.

Back in the detention cell corridor, Luke told the others the bad news: "There isn't any other way out."

More laserfire sailed through the corridor, some blasts impacting dangerously close to Luke and his allies. Han edged out from his alcove, fired back at the stormtroopers, then said, "I can't hold them off forever! Now what?"

"This is some rescue," Leia said sarcastically. "When you came in here, didn't you have a plan for getting out?"

Han gestured to Luke and said, "*He's* the brains, sweetheart."

Luke said, "Well, I didn't . . ."

Leia grabbed Luke's blaster rifle and fired at a small grate in the wall next to Han. The blast tore a hole through the mesh, and Han felt the force of the explosion against the leggings of his stormtrooper armour. He shouted, "What the hell are you doing?"

"Somebody has to save our skins," Leia said, then tossed Luke's rifle back to him. "Into the garbage chute, flyboy." She jumped through the narrow opening she'd created in the grate.

Chewbacca and Han exchanged amazed glances. Neither had expected the princess to be so resourceful, let alone be bold enough to leap into a garbage chute. Chewbacca moved toward the shattered grate, then recoiled from it and yowled.

"Get in there!" Han yelled. "Get in there, you big furry oaf! I don't care what you smell! Get in there and don't worry about it." He gave Chewbacca a big kick, and the Wookiee disappeared into the tiny opening. Then Han turned to Luke and said, "Wonderful girl!

Either I'm going to kill her or I'm beginning to like her. Get in there!"

Han continued firing back at the stormtroopers while Luke ducked laserfire and jumped through the hole. Han fired a few more blasts to create a smoky cover, then held his blaster forward as he dived into the chute.

He yelled all the way down. Like the others who'd preceded him, he landed in a deep pile of garbage.

The garbage room was a metal-walled chamber that contained heaps of trash, everything from broken metal beams and bits of plastic scrap to organic waste. A pool of foul-smelling muck completely covered the floor. Leia's white gown and Luke's stormtrooper armour were already plastered with grime, and Chewbacca's fur was matted with swill.

Han leered at Leia and said, "The garbage chute was a really wonderful idea. What an incredible smell you've discovered!" Seeing Chewbacca trying to open a metal hatch, Han drew his blaster and said, "Let's get out of here! Get away from there."

Luke shouted, "No! Wait!"

Too late. Han fired at the hatch, and the laserbolt ricocheted wildly around the metal-walled chamber. Everyone dived for cover until the fired bolt's charge ended in a small explosion that didn't even dent the metal wall.

"Will you forget it?" Luke shouted to Han. "I already tried it." Gesturing to the hatch, he added, "It's magnetically sealed."

Livid at Han, Leia tilted her chin at his blaster and said, "Put that thing away! You're going to get us all killed."

"Absolutely, Your Worship," Han replied. "Look, I had everything under control until you led us down here. You know, it's not going to take them long to figure out what happened to us."

"It could be worse," Leia said.

Unexpectedly, a loud, inhuman moan worked its way up from the mucky pool. The moan echoed off the garbage room walls.

Chewbacca turned to a wall and cowered. Despite the hazard posed by the magnetically sealed walls, Luke and Han held their blasters out, ready to fire. Han said, "It's worse."

Luke said, "There's something alive in here!"

"That's your imagination," Han said.

"Something just moved past my leg!" Luke reported, then glimpsed a thick, serpent-like body twist through the muck. Luke pointed and said, "Look! Did you see that?"

"What?" Han asked.

They all looked down around their feet. No one saw the single eyestalk that rose like a periscope from the muck. The eye belonged to a dianoga, an omnivorous seven-tentacled predator that had wound up on the Death Star quite by accident. The dianoga's eye quickly surveyed the four figures who appeared to be a tasty alternative to garbage. Then the eyestalk submerged.

Suddenly, Luke was yanked under the muck.

Han shouted, "Kid! Luke!" He pushed aside some garbage, but there wasn't any sign of Luke's armoured body. "Luke!" He reached into the muck but couldn't get his grip on anything. Precious seconds ticked by, and Han, Leia and Chewbacca became more anxious. Han shouted again, "Luke!"

There was an explosion of muck as Luke broke the surface, gasping for air. A membraned tentacle was wrapped around his head, and Luke thrashed and struggled against the creature's hold.

"Luke!" Leia cried out. She grabbed a long metal pipe, extended it, and yelled, "Luke, Luke, grab hold of this!"

"Blast it, will you!" Luke yelled. "My gun's jammed."

Not knowing where to shoot and afraid he might hit Luke, Han said, "Where?"

"Anywhere!" Luke hollered. Han fired downward, but the creature held Luke tight. He fired two more blasts.

"Oh!" Luke shouted, then he was pulled under again.

Han called out, "Luke! Luke!"

Without warning, the walls of the garbage room

shuddered, then went quiet. Han and Leia exchanged a worried look.

What now? Leia wondered.

With a rush of bubbles, Luke bobbed up through the muck.

"Help him!" Leia yelled as Han scrambled through the trash to lift Luke to his feet. Hoping Luke knew the cause of the walls shuddering, Leia asked, "What happened?"

"I don't know," Luke gasped. "It just let go of me and disappeared."

Han looked around at the walls and said, "I got a bad feeling about this."

The walls rumbled again, but this time they pushed inward.

"The walls are moving!" Luke shouted, then realised, *This room is a trash compactor!*

"Don't just stand there," Leia said to Han. "Try and brace it with something. Help me!"

They reached for discarded metal beams and tube-like poles, then angled them between the closing walls. Because all the garbage kept shifting and pushing up around them, it was difficult work. Despite their efforts, the poles snapped and the beams bent, and the walls continued to close in.

"Wait a minute!" Luke cried, and reached for his comlink transmitter. "See-Threepio. Come in,

See-Threepio! See-Threepio!" When no answer came, Luke said, "Where could he be?"

C-3PO had accidentally left his comlink transmitter on top of a computer console in the command office for Docking Bay 327, which still contained the *Millennium Falcon*. Fortunately, when the stormtroopers finally shattered the lock and burst into the office, their attention was immediately drawn to the motionless bodies of the gantry officer and his aide lying on the floor, and they didn't notice the comlink transmitter.

The stormtrooper squad leader gestured at the abandoned computer station and said to one trooper, "Take over!" Directing another trooper's attention to the gantry officer's body, he commanded, "See to him!" Then the squad leader noticed the office's supply-cabinet door was closed and said, "Look, there!"

A trooper pushed a button and the supply cabinet slid open, revealing C-3PO and R2-D2. The stormtroopers had no idea that the droids had deliberately locked themselves inside.

"They're madmen!" C-3PO exclaimed. "They're heading for the prison level. If you hurry, you might catch them." The protocol droid knew Luke and the others had already escaped from the prison level, and hoped his ruse would distract the stormtroopers.

Believing that the droids were victims and not allies of the invaders, the stormtrooper squad leader turned to five troopers and said, "Follow me!" To one other, he ordered, "You stand guard." The squad leader and five troopers ran out of the command office.

"Come on!" C-3PO said to R2-D2, but when they moved away from the supply cabinet, the remaining trooper raised his blaster rifle at them. Thinking fast, C-3PO faced the trooper and said, "Oh! All this excitement has overrun the circuits in my counterpart here. If you don't mind, I'd like to take him down to maintenance."

"All right," the trooper said with a nod.

C-3PO and R2-D2 hurried out of the office.

"See-Threepio!" Luke shouted into his comlink as the garbage room walls continued to rumble closer. "Come in, See-Threepio! See-Threepio!"

Chewbacca whined and pushed against one of the walls with his large paws. Han and Leia worked together, trying to brace a long pole between the contracting walls. All around them, garbage was snapping and popping as it was pushed together.

Leia began to slip down into the trash. Han placed his hands on Leia's hips and lifted her as he said, "Get to the top!"

"I can't," Leia said, but managed with Han's help.

Luke hung on to the comlink transmitter and tried to contact C-3PO again. "Where could he be? See-Threepio? See-Threepio, will you come in?"

After eluding the stormtroopers in the command office, R2-D2 and C-3PO returned to Docking Bay 327, where they took protective cover behind some barrels. C-3PO moved cautiously to see the *Millennium Falcon* still resting on the hangar deck. A group of stormtroopers exited the *Falcon*, carrying the bodies of the scanning crew and the two troopers who'd unwittingly donated their armour to Luke and Han. Five stormtroopers remained on guard beside the *Falcon*'s landing ramp. There was no sign of Luke and the others.

C-3PO turned to R2-D2, who stood beside a computer service panel that was embedded in a wall. "They aren't here!" said the golden droid with dismay. "Something must have happened to them." He gestured at the service panel and said, "See if they've been captured."

R2-D2 extended his computer interface arm and carefully plugged it into the service panel's socket. A complex array of electronic sounds spewed from the astromech's head.

Impatient and filled with worry, C-3PO cried, "Hurry!"

✦

In the garbage room, the converging walls were less than two metres apart and still closing. Luke, Leia, Han and Chewbacca struggled to avoid being crushed as they climbed the shifting heaps of trash.

"One thing's for sure," Han said. "We're all going to be a lot thinner!" Seeing that Leia was losing her footing, he shouted, "Get on top of it!"

"I'm trying!" Leia shouted back.

Luke thought, *Is this how we're going to die?!* He kept his comlink activated, but with the walls now barely a metre apart, the possibility of C-3PO being able to help was a hope that was fading fast.

R2-D2 searched the Death Star's computer banks, but found no record of any intruders being captured since the *Falcon* had arrived in Docking Bay 327. The astromech rotated his dome and beeped his report to C-3PO.

"Thank goodness they haven't found them!" C-3PO said. Glancing at the *Falcon*, he asked, "Where could they be?"

R2-D2 noticed the device that C-3PO had recovered, then beeped and whistled frantically.

"Use the comlink?" C-3PO replied, then realised he was still holding the transmitter. "Oh, my! I forgot . . . I turned it off!" He activated the comlink and said, "Are you there, sir?"

"See-Threepio!" Luke answered.

C-3PO said, "We've had some problems —"

"Will you shut up and listen to me," Luke interrupted. "Shut down all the garbage mashers on the detention level, will you? Do you copy? Shut down all the garbage mashers on the detention level."

Inside the garbage room, the walls didn't stop moving, and only seconds remained before they'd meet. Fearing C-3PO hadn't heard him, Luke repeated, "Shut down all the garbage mashers on the detention level."

R2-D2 beeped a question to C-3PO, who replied, "No. Shut them all down! Hurry!"

R2-D2's extension arm twisted in the computer socket, then he and C-3PO listened to the comlink. They'd hoped to hear that all was well, but instead, the droids heard their friends screaming.

Holding the comlink away from his head, C-3PO looked at R2-D2 and cried, "Listen to them! They're dying, Artoo-Detoo!"

CHAPTER 11

HEARING more screams, C-3PO said mournfully, "Curse my metal body! I wasn't fast enough. It's all my fault! My poor master!"

But then, from the comlink, Luke's excited voice said, "See-Threepio, we're all right!"

Inside the narrow confines of the garbage room, the hollering continued, not because of injury but from the sheer joy that everyone was still alive and unharmed. Holding his comlink, Luke sat atop a pile of trash and communicated to C-3PO, "We're all right. You did great."

Chewbacca howled with relief. Despite themselves, Han and Leia embraced.

Luke saw a hatch against the far wall. To C-3PO, he said, "Hey . . . hey, open the pressure maintenance hatch on unit number . . ." He turned to Han and asked, "Where are we?"

Han checked numbers that were etched on the hatch and read aloud, "Three two six three eight two-seven."

C-3PO made sure R2-D2 heard the numbers correctly, and the astromech opened the hatch.

Darth Vader may have sensed Obi-Wan's presence on the Death Star, but not a single Imperial officer, stormtrooper or droid noticed Obi-Wan's stealthy movement through the corridors as he made his way to the nearest generator trench.

Ben stepped through a doorway and surveyed the trench. It was formed by two incredibly steep facing walls, and the air between them was taut with high-voltage electricity. A narrow bridge without guardrails spanned the trench, and an even narrower footbridge – only centimetres wide, and also without guardrails – extended from the bridge's side to wrap around a power terminal. The power terminal stood atop a cylindrical generator tower. From the schematics that R2-D2 had conjured up back at the command station, Ben knew he'd have to step onto the footbridge to reach the generator's control panels, and that the generator tower was many kilometres tall.

Even for a Jedi Knight, that was a long way down.

Focused on his mission and fearless of the dizzying height, Ben moved across the bridge, then onto the footbridge. He edged carefully around the power terminal until he could reach the generator controls. He pressed one lever, then edged farther around the terminal until he found the controls for the tractor beam power coupling.

The hatch for trash compactor 32-6-3827 adjoined a dusty, unused hallway. Han and Luke had removed their stormtrooper armour but retained the troopers' white utility belts, each of which carried blaster power cell containers, a tool kit and a grappling hook attached to a fibercord reel. Chewbacca sat outside the open hatch and tried to brush the grime from his matted fur. Leia smoothed out her gown and checked the pins that held her hair in place.

Handing a blaster rifle to Luke, Han glanced at Leia and said, "If we can just avoid any more female advice, we ought to be able to get out of here."

Luke said, "Well, let's get moving!"

A loud, angry moan drifted out from the open hatch. Evidently, the dianoga had survived in the garbage room and was now even more hungry. The noise caused Chewbacca to jump and run away from the hatch.

"Where are you going?" Han said, glaring at the Wookiee. Embarrassed by his copilot's behaviour, Han turned toward the hatch and raised his blaster.

"No, wait," Leia said urgently. "They'll hear!"

Too late again. Han fired the blaster at the hatch,

and the noise echoed throughout the hallway. Disgusted by Han's thoughtless action, Luke shook his head.

"Come here, you big coward!" Han called to the Wookiee, who stood trembling beside a nearby stack of barrels. "Chewie! Come here!"

Leia fixed her furious gaze on Han and said, "Listen. I don't know who you are or where you came from, but from now on, you do as I tell you. OK?" She walked past Han and began to lead the group through the hallway, but Chewbacca fell into step just in front of her.

Catching up beside Leia, Han said, "Look, Your Worshipfulness, let's get one thing straight! I take orders from just one person! Me!"

"It's a wonder you're still alive," Leia said. Glaring at Chewbacca, she added, "Will somebody get this big walking carpet out of my way?" She brushed past the Wookiee.

Han shook his head and muttered, "No reward is worth this."

Ben was about to remove himself from his perilous perch upon the footbridge that ringed the generator tower's power terminal when he heard footsteps approaching. He quickly readjusted a lever on the power terminal so any passer-by wouldn't notice his sabotage, then braced his body against the terminal, concealing himself from the bridge that spanned the trench.

A detachment of stormtroopers entered through a doorway and stepped onto the bridge. The commanding officer turned to two troopers and said, "Give me regular reports, please."

"Right," replied one trooper. The two troopers remained near the doorway by which they'd arrived while the other troopers marched across the bridge and through the facing doorway.

Ben intended to exit the trench by the same route. As he readjusted the lever to shut down the tractor beam, he overheard the nearby troopers speaking.

"Do you know what's going on?" asked the first trooper.

"Maybe it's another drill," the second replied.

Ben moved cautiously on the footbridge and peered around the power terminal. The two troopers were still near the far doorway, facing each other. The first trooper said, "Have you seen that new BT-sixteen?"

The second trooper said, "Yeah, some of the other guys were telling me about it. They say it's quite a thing to –"

Using the Force, Ben flexed his fingers and gestured at the two troopers. Both suddenly heard – or thought they heard – a muffled explosion from the doorway behind them, and turned away from the power terminal.

"What was that?" asked the second trooper.

"That's nothing," said the first trooper. "Outgassing. Don't worry about it."

Neither noticed Ben step onto the bridge and exit the generator trench.

Luke, Leia, Han and Chewbacca entered a corridor that was on the same level as the command office for Docking Bay 327. Arriving at a window that overlooked the hangar, Han gazed down at the *Millennium Falcon* and said, "There she is."

Luke looked through the window and counted five stormtrooper sentries outside the *Falcon*. There was no sign of R2-D2 or C-3PO. Luke switched on his comlink transmitter and said, "See-Threepio, do you copy?"

"Yes, sir," C-3PO answered.

"Are you safe?" Luke asked.

"For the moment," the droid replied. "We're in the main hangar across from the ship."

"We're right above you," Luke said. "Stand by."

Leia tugged at Han's sleeve and gestured at the *Falcon*. "You came in that thing?" she said. "You're braver than I thought."

"Nice!" Han was thoroughly exasperated. "Come on!"

They walked fast down a hallway, making their way to the lift-tube that would take them to the lower level. Han made sweeping movements with his blaster rifle, ready to fire at the first sign of trouble. But, as the group rounded a corner, even Han was surprised to run straight into seven approaching stormtroopers.

"It's them!" shouted the squad leader. "Blast them!"

Han's blaster rifle was already levelled at the squad leader, and he didn't hesitate to fire. The blast knocked the squad leader off his feet and the six remaining troopers stumbled back. Without any plan but to knock down every Imperial soldier in sight, Han fired again and charged the startled troopers, who turned and ran back up the hallway. As Han chased and fired after the troopers, he shouted to his allies, "Get back to the ship!"

"Where are you going?" Luke yelled as Chewbacca ran after Han. "Come back!"

Watching Han's departure, Leia said, "He certainly has courage."

"What good will it do us if he gets himself killed?" Luke took Leia's hand. "Come on!" They ran off in the other direction down the hallway.

Hollering and firing his blaster rifle, Han chased the stormtroopers through a long subhallway. At the end, the troopers were forced to turn left round a corner. Not thinking about where the turn might lead, Han ran after the troopers and entered a TIE fighter hangar.

Han stopped in his tracks. The hangar was filled with hundreds of stormtroopers, and it appeared that he had interrupted their weapons drill. The stormtroopers he'd been chasing now stopped and turned with their blasters raised. The other troopers all looked his way. Han squeezed off a shot to fell one more trooper, then turned and ran for his life.

Chewbacca had been trying to catch up with Han when he heard the hail of blasterfire up ahead, then saw Han come racing back toward him. A hail of laserbolts slammed into the wall behind Han as he ran past. Quickly sizing up the situation, the Wookiee turned and ran even faster after him.

Before Luke and Leia could reach the hangar that contained the *Millennium Falcon*, they were spotted by yet another squad of stormtroopers. Luke fired his blaster rifle wildly as he and Leia rushed down a narrow subhallway, trying to elude the troopers who now fired at them from behind.

The subhallway ended at a short ramp that led up to an open doorway. Luke and Leia raced up the ramp and were through the doorway before they realised the floor ended at an enormous air shaft. Luke nearly lost his balance at the edge of the floor, but Leia grabbed hold of his arm and pulled him back.

"I think we took a wrong turn," Luke said, and heard his words echo as he surveyed the air shaft. The shaft's steep walls seemed to stretch to infinity. Across the chasm, another open doorway was set in the facing wall. Luke and Leia realised they were standing upon nothing more than a shallow overhang that housed a retractable bridge.

Blasterfire exploded behind them. Luke turned and fired at the advancing stormtroopers. Leia found a control panel that was embedded in the doorway. She reached to the panel, hit a switch, and the door slid shut behind them.

"There's no lock!" Leia said.

Luke aimed his blaster at the control panel and fired, frying the door's opening mechanisms. He said, "That oughta hold them for a while."

Looking to the doorway on the other side of the shaft, Leia said, "Quick, we've got to get across. Find the controls that extend the bridge."

Luke looked at the smouldering circuits on the panel in the doorway. "Oh," he said, "I think I just blasted it."

There came a grinding sound from the door behind them. Leia warned, "They're coming through!"

Luke thought, *There's got to be a way out of this!* Looking up, he spotted an outcropping of large metal pipes that jutted down from above. Then he remembered: *My stormtrooper utility belt has a grappling hook.* But as he reached to the belt, laserfire hit the wall behind him.

Luke and Leia fell back against the doorway's alcove as more laserbolts whizzed past them. Glancing out from the alcove, they saw three stormtroopers firing from an upper-level doorway on the facing wall. Luke braced himself, aimed up at the troopers and fired back.

One trooper was hit in the chest and fell forward into the shaft. The other troopers returned fire, and Luke threw himself back beside Leia in the alcove.

"Here, hold this," Luke said, handing the blaster rifle to Leia.

Leia bravely repeated Luke's movements, stepping out from the alcove to exchange fire with the stormtroopers before ducking back. While she kept the troopers occupied, Luke pulled the grappling hook from his belt. He was still paying out the hook's thin cable when the door behind him began to open.

"Here they come!" Leia shouted. She fired again at the stormtroopers across the shaft. One of her shots struck a trooper, and he collapsed.

Luke tossed the hook high, letting its weight carry the cable up to the metal pipes. The hook whipped around one pipe and the hook's tines locked onto the cable. Luke gave the cable a single tug to make sure it was secure, then pulled Leia to his side. Behind them, the door opened a fraction more.

Leia kissed Luke's cheek and said, "For luck!"

Keeping her grip on the blaster rifle, Leia wrapped her arms around Luke as he pushed off from the overhang. They swung across the treacherous shaft and alighted on the opposite ledge, just as the stormtroopers broke through and fired at them from behind.

Leia returned fire, then she and Luke scrambled through the doorway and ran into another hallway. This time, they wouldn't get lost on their way back to the *Falcon*.

Several stormtroopers rushed through a Death Star hallway. One trooper reported, "We think they may be splitting up. They may be on levels five and six now, sir."

Ben stood in the shadows of a narrow passageway that adjoined the hallway. When he was sure the troopers had passed, he drew his lightsaber from his belt. He did not activate the blade but held it ready. He had a feeling he would be using his weapon sooner than later. Much sooner.

C-3PO was becoming increasingly worried as he and R2-D2 waited for their allies to arrive in the docking bay. "Where could they be?" the protocol droid asked.

R2-D2 plugged into the computer socket and responded with a beep. He didn't know either.

Han and Chewbacca raced through a corridor with several stormtroopers hot on their trail. As the man and Wookiee approached a wide doorway, a trooper shouted out from behind, "Close the blast doors!"

Suddenly, thick metal doors began to slide out from the doorway's frame. Chewbacca maintained a breakneck pace as he ran between the converging doors. Han span and fired back at the stormtroopers, then turned again and leaped through the closing aperture at the last possible moment before the blast doors sealed off the corridor behind him.

"Open the blast doors!" shouted the trooper. "Open the blast doors!"

On the other side, Han and Chewbacca kept running.

Ben still had his lightsaber drawn as he moved along through an access tunnel that led back to Docking Bay 327. Having disabled the tractor beam, his remaining goal was to make sure Luke and Princess Leia left the Death Star on the *Millennium Falcon*. But before he could reach the hangar, he sighted a tall, shadowy form at the end of the tunnel.

It was his former apprentice, Darth Vader.

Vader had already activated the red blade of his lightsaber. For a moment, he stood motionless. Then he approached Ben.

Obi-Wan activated his own lightsaber and stepped slowly forward. He'd fought Vader before. He hadn't been afraid then either.

CHAPTER 12

"I'VE been waiting for you, Obi-Wan," Vader said as he moved closer to the elderly Jedi Knight. "We meet again, at last. The circle is now complete."

Obi-Wan assumed an offensive position.

Vader continued, "When I left you, I was but the learner; now I am the master."

"Only a master of evil, Darth," Obi-Wan said. He made a sudden lunge at Vader, but the dark lord blocked the attack. There was a loud electric crackle as their lightsabers made contact. Obi-Wan swung again and again, but each time Vader parried.

Vader said, "Your powers are weak, old man."

"You can't win, Darth," Obi-Wan said. "If you strike me down, I shall become more powerful than you can possibly imagine."

"You should not have come back," Vader said.

Their lightsabers clashed again. And again, and again. And as their battle continued, they moved closer to the main doorway that led directly to the hangar that contained the *Millennium Falcon*.

Chewbacca and Han ran through a hallway until they arrived at a side door to the hangar that housed their captured ship. Bracing themselves against the wall, they peered into the hangar and saw the same five stormtrooper sentries they'd seen earlier from the window at the upper level. The *Falcon* looked the same as they'd left it, with the landing ramp still down.

"Didn't we just leave this party?" Han said. He glanced to his left and saw Leia and Luke rushing up from the other end of the hallway. When they arrived at his side, he said, "What kept you?"

"We ran into some old friends," Leia replied, catching her breath.

Luke asked, "Is the ship all right?"

"Seems OK, if we can get to it," Han answered. "Just hope the old man got the tractor beam out of commission."

Han was trying to think of a way to get rid of the stormtroopers in the hangar when Luke said, "Look!" Inexplicably, the stormtroopers trotted away from the *Falcon*'s landing ramp and moved past the deep elevator well.

Inside the hangar, C-3PO also saw the stormtroopers

run to the other side of the elevator well. C-3PO turned to R2-D2 and said, "Come on, Artoo, we're going!"

R2-D2 extended his retractable third tread to the hangar deck and rolled forward after C-3PO, heading for the *Falcon*.

Back in the hallway, Han said, "Now's our chance! Go!"

Chewbacca, Han, Leia and Luke ran for the *Falcon*'s landing ramp. Luke glanced to his right and saw the stormtroopers had moved to the other side of the elevator well. They faced away from him, their attention having been drawn to a fight that was taking place in the hallway beyond the main doorway.

It was a lightsaber duel. Luke could only imagine the identity of the tall, black-clad humanoid who wielded a red lightsaber. The other duellist wore a brown cloak, and Luke recognised him immediately.

"Ben?" Luke said, and came to a stop. *Who's he fighting?*

Ben looked to Luke and smiled, then he raised his lightsaber before him and closed his eyes. He looked almost serene.

Darth Vader thought Obi-Wan was surrendering, but the dark lord was without mercy. Vader's lightsaber swept through the air and sliced through Ben's form. Ben's cloak and lightsaber fell to the floor. His body was gone.

"No!" Luke shouted.

Hearing Luke's cry, the stormtroopers turned and shot at him. Luke raised his blaster rifle and returned their fire, hitting one trooper, who tumbled forward into the elevator well.

Han immediately joined in the fight, firing at the troopers while the droids and Chewbacca hurried into the *Falcon*. "Come on!" Han shouted to Luke.

Darth Vader ignored the blaster-fight and looked down at the old brown cloak and lightsaber that lay on the floor. Incredibly, Obi-Wan had completely disappeared. *Where is he? How could he vanish? What sort of trickery is this?* He had assumed Obi-Wan's study of the Force had ended long ago, and that his powers had diminished over time. But Vader was wrong.

Luke and Han kept firing at the troopers. Another was shot down. Leia shouted, "Come on! Come on! Luke, it's too late!"

Darth Vader looked away from Obi-Wan's cloak, then turned and strode toward the doorway to the hangar.

Han shouted, "Blast the door, kid!"

Luke fired at the controls beside the doorway, then two blast doors slid out from the walls to seal off the passage before Vader could enter the hangar. Han and Leia ran into the *Falcon*. The three remaining stormtroopers continued to fire at Luke. Luke fired again, and reduced their number to two.

Then, from out of nowhere, Luke heard Ben's voice: "Run, Luke! Run!"

Luke looked around, trying to see where the voice had come from. He saw nothing, but chose to heed Ben's words and raced into the *Falcon*.

Chewbacca already had the ship's sub-light engines started when Han rushed into the cockpit. Han stowed his blaster rifle, jumped into the pilot's seat and said, "I hope the old man got that tractor beam out of commission, or this is going to be a real short trip. OK, hit it!"

The Wookiee punched the controls. The *Falcon* launched out of the hangar in reverse, then spun and blasted away from the Death Star.

In the *Falcon*'s main hold, the droids looked at Luke, who sat at the game table with a blank expression. Leia carried a blanket over to Luke, wrapped it around his shoulders, and sat beside him. Luke just stared at the centre of the game table. *Why didn't Ben defend himself? Why?*

In the cockpit, Chewbacca was still waiting for the nav computer to come up with a route into hyperspace when Han spotted four blips on a sensor scope. "We're coming up on their sentry ships," Han said. "Hold 'em off! Angle the deflector shields while I charge up the main guns!"

Chewbacca threw switches to adjust the shields. Han pulled on a pair of skin-tight leather piloting gloves and bolted out of the cockpit.

Back in the main hold, Leia continued to sit by Luke. He shook his head sadly and said, "I can't believe he's gone."

R2-D2 emitted a sympathetic beep. Although C-3PO was rarely at a loss for words, he remained silent.

Leia said, "There wasn't anything you could have done."

Just then, Han rushed into the hold. Looking at Luke, he said, "Come on, buddy, we're not out of this yet!"

Leia and Luke jumped up from their seats, leaving the droids at the game table. While Leia ran to the *Falcon*'s cockpit, Luke shrugged off the blanket that Leia had given him and followed Han to the access hatch for the gunport turrets.

The access hatch opened to a narrow passage tube with a ladder that travelled between the dorsal and ventral quad laser cannons. Han climbed up the ladder and Luke climbed down. Each arrived in a windowed gunner's enclosure that contained a manoeuvrable seat with firing controls and targeting instrumentation. Outside each window was a large swivel-mounted quad laser cannon. Luke was pretty sure the cannons were military issue. *I don't even want to think how Han got these weapons!*

Luke and Han settled into their seats at each end of the passage tube. Han adjusted his comlink headset and spoke into the attached microphone: "You in, kid? OK, stay sharp!"

Luke quickly familiarised himself with the controls. There was a targeting computer that worked in conjunction with the *Falcon*'s navigational computer and sensor array to calculate trajectories and attack and intercept courses. Grasping twin firing grips with built-in triggers, Luke shifted his wrists to the right; his seat automatically swivelled to the left, and the cannon's four laser barrels - visible through the ventral window - swung hard to the right. Then he pulled back on the controls and the seat lowered as the cannon raised. Each movement was accompanied by the mechanical whine from the cannon's tracking servos.

Suddenly, the *Falcon* shuddered as its shields took a laser hit from a distant attacker. In the cockpit, Leia and Chewbacca glanced from the scopes to the window, keeping their eyes peeled for the incoming Imperial sentry ships. Chewbacca spotted them first and barked. Leia said into the cockpit's comlink, "Here they come!"

The sentry ships were four TIE fighters. They came in fast, flying in a tight formation toward the *Falcon*'s cockpit before they broke away from each other and fanned out around the freighter. Then the fighters looped back and fired again at their target. Green laserbolts hammered at the *Falcon*'s deflector shields.

The *Falcon* bounced and vibrated and the ship's power surged. In the *Falcon*'s main hold, C-3PO clung to his seat beside R2-D2 as the lights dimmed and then came back on. Hoping to make himself useful, R2-D2 left the game table to inspect the engineering station. Not wanting to be left alone, C-3PO went with him.

A TIE fighter manoeuvred above the *Falcon*. Han tracked the fighter and fired at it with his laser cannon, but missed. The TIE fighter looped back and streaked into Luke's view, and Luke fired too, without effect.

Two TIE fighters spat laserfire and the *Falcon* bounced as it took more hits. Luke hung tight to his controls and fired at one of the passing TIE fighters as it soared past his window. He shouted, "They're coming in too fast!"

C-3PO and R2-D2 stumbled out of the main hold and into the passage tube just as more Imperial laserfire struck the *Falcon*. There was a small explosion at the floor. C-3PO shouted, "Oh!" as he was thrown against the passage tube's wall.

In the cockpit, Leia watched the computer readouts

as Chewbacca manipulated the ship's controls. "We've lost lateral controls," she reported.

Via comlink, Han answered, "Don't worry, she'll hold together."

Near the droids, a control panel blew out in a shower of sparks beside the laser cannon access hatch. Han heard the explosion. Speaking directly to his ship, he said, "You hear me, baby? Hold together!"

R2-D2 hurried over to the smoking, sparking control panel. Among the astromech's many useful devices was a fire extinguisher. He sprayed the control panel until the fire was out.

The TIE fighters continued their attack. Luke and Han swivelled madly in their turrets as they returned fire. Han followed a TIE fighter in his sights and pumped rapid bursts of laserbolts at it. He connected, and the TIE fighter exploded. Han laughed victoriously.

A moment later, another TIE fighter swept into Luke's line of fire. Luke swung the cannon as he squeezed the firing grips and scored a direct hit, shattering the TIE fighter.

"Got him!" Luke shouted back to Han. "I got him!"

Han glanced down the passage tube, waved at Luke and said, "Great, kid!" As he quickly returned his attention to his own targeting computer he added, "Don't get cocky."

From the cockpit, Leia reported, "There are still two more of them out there!"

The two remaining TIE fighters crossed in front of the *Falcon*, then veered away to attack from different directions. Han swivelled in his chair and followed one TIE fighter with blasts from his cannon, and Luke did the same as the other fighter streaked under the *Falcon*.

Both TIE fighters looped back, firing more rounds of green laserbolts. One angled into Luke's view, and he fired a laserblast at it. The fighter exploded.

The last of the attacking TIE fighters zoomed in and fired at the top of the *Falcon*. Han swivelled behind his laser cannon and squeezed the firing grips. The fighter was instantly consumed in a massive, fiery explosion. Han blew out a relieved breath.

Luke laughed. "That's it! We did it!"

In the cockpit, Leia embraced Chewbacca and said, "We did it!"

"Help!" cried C-3PO from a tangle of sparking wires on the floor of the passage tube. "I think I'm melting!" Sighting R2-D2, he added, "This is all your fault."

R2-D2 beeped in disagreement.

The nav computer found a hyperspace solution and Chewbacca seized the opportunity to gain more distance from the Death Star. He punched the controls, and the *Falcon* blasted into hyperspace.

✦

Darth Vader stood with Grand Moff Tarkin in the Death Star control room. Tarkin looked at the wide viewscreen and said, "Are they away?"

"They have just made the jump into hyperspace," Vader said.

"You're sure the homing beacon is secure aboard their ship?" Tarkin said.

Vader didn't answer. He'd already told Tarkin that the homing beacon had been placed on the Corellian freighter and did not feel compelled to repeat himself. It had been Vader's idea to use the rescue of Princess Leia to the Empire's advantage. It had also been his idea to send the TIE fighters in pursuit of the freighter; if the princess and her allies suspected they'd been allowed to escape, they might not proceed directly to the rebel base. The loss of the four TIE fighters and their pilots was an insignificant price for gaining the base's location.

"I'm taking an awful risk, Vader," Tarkin said. "This had better work."

Again, Vader remained silent, but he thought, *If we'd done things your way, Princess Leia would have been executed by now. And how would that have helped us find the rebel base, Grand Moff Tarkin?*

"Not a bad bit of rescuing, huh!" Han said as he returned to the *Millennium Falcon*'s cockpit, just as Chewbacca rose to leave and check the ship for damage in the aft section. Leia remained seated behind the piloting controls.

Sliding into the Wookiee's vacated seat, Han pulled off his gloves and added, "You know, sometimes I amaze even myself."

"That doesn't sound too hard," Leia said. "They let us go. It's the only explanation for the ease of our escape."

"Easy!" Han said, raising his eyebrows quizzically. "You call that easy?"

"They're tracking us!" Leia insisted.

"Not this ship, sister," Han said.

Let him think what he wants, Leia thought. She said, "At least the information in Artoo-Detoo is still intact."

"What's so important?" Han asked. "What's he carrying?"

"The technical readouts of that battle station," Leia replied. "I only hope that when the data is analysed, a weakness can be found. It's not over yet!"

"It is for me, sister!" Han said angrily. "Look, I ain't in this for your revolution, and I'm not in it for you, Princess. I expect to be well paid. I'm in it for the money!"

Leia glared at Han. "You needn't worry about your reward," she said. "When you get us to our destination, you'll receive it."

"Don't you think it'd help if you told me where we're going?"

"The fourth moon of the planet Yavin," Leia said. "That's where the base is. Then you can do whatever you like. If money is all that you love, then that's what you'll receive."

Han looked out the window. Leia rose from the pilot's seat and turned to leave just as Luke entered the cockpit. Looking at Luke, she said, "Your friend is quite a mercenary. I wonder if he really cares about anything . . . or anybody." She walked out.

"*I* care!" Luke said, but Leia was already walking back to the main hold. Luke shook his head and sat down in the pilot's seat. Then he looked at Han and asked, "So . . . what do you think of her, Han?"

"I'm not trying to, kid!" Han replied.

Under his breath, Luke said, "Good."

Han glanced at Luke, who'd turned his attention to the ship's controls. Realising that Luke might have feelings for the princess, Han decided to have some fun. He said, "Still, she's got a lot of spirit. I don't know, what do you think? Do you think a princess and a guy like me –"

"No!" Luke said sharply, then looked away, glowering.

Han grinned. Now he *knew* Luke had feelings for Leia.

While checking the nav computer calculations for the journey to Yavin's fourth moon, Han wondered if anyone - with or without the precious technical readouts - would be able to destroy the Death Star.

He doubted it very much.

CHAPTER 13

THE planet Yavin was an orange gas giant, nearly 200,000 kilometres in diameter. It had dozens of moons, three of which could support humanoid life. The innermost habitable moon was designated Yavin 4, and was covered by steamy jungles and volcanic mountain ranges. Yavin 4 had once been home to an ancient civilisation called the Massassi; all that remained were scattered ruins, including a towering ziggurat – a terraced pyramid with successively receding stories – known as the Great Temple. It was in this long-abandoned structure that the Alliance – following their evacuation from the planet Dantooine – had relocated their primary base.

After the *Millennium Falcon* was cleared for landing, a rebel sentry visually monitored the freighter's atmospheric descent from an observation tower, which was little more than a barrel-topped pole extending high above the jungle floor. The *Falcon* touched down near the Great Temple, where rebel troops greeted Princess Leia and her rescuers.

Two military speeders transported Luke and the others into the main hangar deck, a large chamber that had been excavated from the lower level of the Great Temple. The hangar contained a few dozen single-pilot starships, mostly T-65 X-wing starfighters but also some older Y-wings. The X-wings were named for their two sets of double-layered wings, which were closed during normal space flight but deployed into an X formation for combat; the end of each wingtip sported a sleek laser cannon. The Y-wing starfighters were distinguished by a forward cockpit module that housed the pilot and the weapons systems, and had two ion jet engines that swept back from the main body. Both X-wing and Y-wing designs included a socket behind the cockpit where an R2 astromech could be inserted to handle all astrogation duties.

The two military speeders came to a stop inside the hangar. The group was then approached by Commander Vanden Willard, a grey-haired leader of the rebel forces on Yavin 4. Willard welcomed Leia with a hug and said, "You're safe! When we heard about Alderaan, we feared the worst."

"We have no time for sorrows, Commander," Leia said. As rebel technicians unloaded R2-D2 from the lead speeder, Leia added, "You must use the information in this Artoo unit to help plan the attack. It's our only hope."

R2-D2 was taken immediately to a computer console and debriefed. The stolen technical readouts were intact. An older, bearded rebel general named Jan Dodonna methodically analysed the data, searching the Death Star's design for the weakness that rebel intelligence had reported to him. If there were indeed a way to strike at the battle station's reactor module, General Dodonna was determined to find it.

Incredibly, he did.

On the Death Star, Darth Vader stood behind a chair in the conference room and watched Grand Moff Tarkin respond to a signal from the comlink on the large round table. Tarkin pressed a button and said, "Yes."

Over the comlink intercom, a voice reported, "*We are approaching the planet Yavin. The rebel base is on a moon on the far side. We are preparing to orbit the planet.*"

On Yavin 4, Luke was still wearing his clothes from Tatooine when he joined the orange-uniformed rebel pilots who gathered in the base's war room briefing area. Commander Willard had told Luke that the Alliance was short of experienced pilots, and Luke had volunteered on the spot. Because the controls of T-16 skyhoppers were similar to those of the X-wing starfighters, Luke had been assigned an X-wing. Luke sat beside another pilot, a dark-haired young man who introduced himself as Wedge Antilles. C-3PO, R2-D2 and some other astromechs stood behind Luke and Wedge. Wondering if there was any chance his friend Biggs had made it all the way to Yavin 4 too, Luke looked around the room. He didn't see Biggs, but spotted Han and Chewbacca lurking against the back wall. *I didn't think they'd be here. Maybe they decided to volunteer too!*

All heads turned to the front as Princess Leia, General Dodonna and Commander Willard entered the room. Leia moved to stand beside Jon "Dutch" Vander, leader of Y-wing Gold Squadron. Dodonna stepped before a large rectangular viewscreen and faced the gathered pilots. The viewscreen displayed the technical readouts for the Death Star.

"The battle station is heavily shielded and carries a firepower greater than half the starfleet," Dodonna said. "Its defences are designed around a direct large-scale assault. A small one-man fighter should be able to penetrate the outer defence."

Given the Death Star's firepower, the pilots had a hard time believing they stood any chance against the superweapon. Jon Vander said, "Pardon me for asking, sir, but what good are snubfighters going to be against *that*?"

Dodonna said, "Well, the Empire doesn't consider a small one-man fighter to be any threat, or they'd have a tighter defence. An analysis of the plans provided by Princess Leia has demonstrated a weakness in the battle station."

R2-D2 – happy to have been instrumental in carrying the plans – beeped proudly to a nearby R2 unit.

"The approach will not be easy," Dodonna continued. As the viewscreen displayed a digital representation of the Death Star's equatorial trench, Dodonna said, "You are required to manoeuvre straight down this trench and skim the surface to this point. The target area is only two metres wide. It's a small thermal exhaust port, right below the main port. The shaft leads directly to the reactor system. A precise hit will start a chain reaction which should destroy the station."

On the viewscreen, a simulation showed a starfighter launching a projectile into what appeared to be a small hole on the floor of the Death Star's trench. As the starfighter pulled out and ascended from the trench, the projectile plummeted through a narrow shaft until it reached the reactor core at the very centre of the space station. Then bright lines radiated out from the reactor core and the station's image vanished.

Dodonna continued, "Only a precise hit will set up a

chain reaction. The shaft is ray-shielded, so you'll have to use proton torpedoes."

Dodonna's presentation generated a rumble of mutterings from the pilots. Wedge said, "That's impossible, even for a computer."

"It's not impossible," Luke said. "I used to bull's-eye womp rats in my T-sixteen back home. They're not much bigger than two metres."

"Then man your ships!" Dodonna ordered. "And may the Force be with you!"

The pilots rose from their seats and headed out through the door that led to the hangar. Luke caught Leia looking in his direction. He couldn't tell from her expression whether she was concerned or disappointed. Then he realised she wasn't looking at him but at someone behind him. Luke turned round, expecting to see Han and Chewbacca, but they had already left the room. The droids were still there, and R2-D2 beeped cheerfully to him. Luke looked back to Leia, but now she was gone too, along with the other rebel leaders.

Everything's happening so fast, Luke thought. *I can't believe it was just the other day that I was watching the suns set on Tatooine, wishing I were anywhere but on that moisture farm. And here I am, over halfway across the galaxy, fighting for a cause I believe in. It's great, but . . .*

I wish I didn't feel so alone.

He thought of Ben and Uncle Owen and Aunt Beru, first with sadness for their loss, then with anger at the Empire. Then he thought of the planet Alderaan, and the anger burned even more.

Luke went to get suited up for his mission.

On the Death Star, Grand Moff Tarkin and Darth Vader watched a computer monitor that showed the space station's position in relation to the planet Yavin and the moon Yavin 4. As the planetary diagrams moved over and past each other on the monitor, a voice from the intercom announced, "*Orbiting the planet at maximum velocity. The moon with the rebel base will be in range in thirty minutes.*"

"This will be a day long remembered," Vader said. "It has seen the end of Kenobi. It will soon see the end of the Rebellion."

Tarkin glanced at Vader, then returned his gaze to the monitor. He anticipated with relish delivering the crushing blow to the Rebel Alliance.

C-3PO and R2-D2 went with Luke to the main hangar. Luke was now wearing a bright orange flight suit and carried a helmet adorned with Alliance emblems. In the hangar, flight crews rushed to make last-minute adjustments to the starfighters. Over a loudspeaker, a man's voice said, *"All flight troops, man your stations. All flight troops, man your stations."*

Stepping down to the hangar floor, Luke found Han and Chewbacca loading small boxes onto an armoured military speeder. The boxes contained precious metals, the only form of currency that Han would accept from the Alliance. He appeared to be completely ignoring the activity of the rebel flight crews and pilots.

Eyeing the box in Han's hands, Luke said, "So . . . you got your reward and you're just leaving, then?"

"That's right, yeah!" Han said. "I got some old debts I got to pay off with this stuff. Even if I didn't, you don't think I'd be fool enough to stick around here, do you?"

Luke was silent, but inside, he fumed.

"Why don't you come with us?" Han said. "You're pretty good in a fight. I could use you."

"Come on!" Luke snapped angrily. "Why don't you take a look around? You know what's about to happen, what they're up against. They could use a good pilot like you. You're turning your back on them."

"What good's a reward if you ain't around to use it?" Han said as he loaded another box on the speeder. "Besides, attacking the battle station ain't my idea of courage. It's more like suicide."

"All right," Luke said. "Well, take care of yourself,

Han. I guess that's what you're best at, isn't it?" He turned and started to walk off.

Han hesitated, then called out, "Hey, Luke . . ."

Luke stopped and turned. Then Han, despite himself, said, "May the Force be with you."

Although Luke may have been surprised to hear those words from the same smuggler who'd claimed not to believe in the Force, he didn't show it. He glanced down at the pile of boxes beside Han, then stared back at Solo for a moment before he turned away again.

As Luke walked off, Han caught Chewbacca's gaze and said, "What're you lookin' at?" Han loaded another box onto the speeder and muttered, "I know what I'm doing."

Scowling, Luke headed for his X-wing. Over the hangar's loudspeaker, the controller's voice announced, "*All pilots to your stations. All pilots to your stations.*"

Leia was walking with a group of rebel soldiers when she saw Luke. She went to him and said, "What's wrong?"

"Oh, it's Han!" Luke replied, shaking his head. "I don't know, I really thought he'd change his mind."

"He's got to follow his own path," Leia said. "No one can choose it for him."

Luke looked away. "I only wish Ben were here."

Leia kissed Luke on the cheek, then moved off with the soldiers, heading for the war room.

Luke found his X-wing. C-3PO and R2-D2 were beside the starfighter, and two technicians were preparing to hoist R2-D2 up to the starfighter's astromech socket. Luke was about to climb up the ladder to the cockpit when he heard a familiar voice call out, "Hey, Luke!"

Luke turned to face his best friend from Tatooine. "Biggs!" he shouted with surprise. Biggs was taller and slightly older than Luke, with dark hair and a moustache. Like Luke, he wore a rebel pilot's uniform and carried a helmet.

"Hey-ay-ay!" Biggs laughed, wrapping an arm around Luke's shoulder.

"I don't believe it!" Luke said.

"How are you?"

"Great!"

Biggs looked from Luke to the X-wing and asked, "You're coming up with us?"

"I'll be right up there with you," Luke replied with a grin. "And have I got some stories to tell you!"

Just then, a deep voice called out, "Skywalker!" Luke and Biggs stopped talking and turned to face Garven Dreis, a veteran pilot and the leader of Red Squadron, the X-wing unit that included Luke and Biggs. Dreis looked sceptically at Luke, then gestured to the X-wing and said, "You sure you can handle this ship?"

Before Luke could answer, Biggs said, "Sir, Luke is the best bush pilot in the Outer Rim territories."

Apparently, that was good enough for Dreis. He grinned at Luke and said, "You'll do all right."

"Thank you, sir," Luke said. "I'll try."

Dreis walked off to another X-wing. Biggs saw that his own craft was ready for lift-off and said, "I've got to get aboard. Listen, you'll tell me your stories when we come back. All right?" He started to head off.

"Biggs," Luke said, and his friend stopped and turned. Beaming with pride, Luke continued, "I told you I'd make it someday."

"Be like old times, Luke," Biggs said. "They'll never stop us!" Biggs walked fast to his starfighter.

As Luke climbed up the ladder to his own X-wing, he looked to the two crewmen who were about to ease R2-D2 into the astromech socket. The crew chief said, "That R2 unit of yours seems a bit beat-up. Do you want a new one?"

"Not on your life!" Luke said. "That little droid and I have been through a lot together." Luke looked directly at the plucky astromech and said, "You OK, Artoo-Detoo?"

R2-D2 beeped enthusiastically.

"Good!" Luke said as he hopped into the cockpit and pulled on his helmet.

"OK, easy!" said the crew chief as R2-D2 was lowered into his snug socket.

Still standing beside the X-wing, C-3PO looked up

to R2-D2 and said, "Hang on tight, Artoo, you've got to come back."

R2-D2 beeped in agreement.

The protocol droid said, "You wouldn't want my life to get boring, would you?"

R2-D2 whistled his reply. The crewmen made some final adjustments, then climbed down to the hangar floor. Luke lowered his cockpit canopy and his X-wing lifted off to a low hover. As he followed the other starfighters toward the wide doorway, he felt a twinge of fear about his mission. *Do we really have any chance of defeating the Death Star?*

Then, from out of nowhere, Ben's disembodied voice said, "*Luke, the Force will be with you.*"

Luke took a deep breath and guided the X-wing out of the hangar.

Outside the ancient Massassi temple, a rebel sentry watched the starfighters rise up over the jungle and race into the morning sky.

Leia and C-3PO proceeded to the war room, where technicians and controllers monitored their illuminated tactical screens. Over the intercom, a robotic voice announced, "*Standby alert. Death Star approaching. Estimated time to firing range, fifteen minutes.*"

Leia knew that Tarkin would order the destruction

of Yavin 4 without any hesitation, just as he had done to Alderaan. *What if the rebel pilots aren't able to carry out General Dodonna's plan?* She tried to push the thought out of her head. *We must succeed. We* must!

CHAPTER 14

LEAVING Yavin 4's atmosphere, the X-wing and Y-wing starfighters sped away across space. They flew in a tight formation at sub-light speed, staying in sight of one another. After they wrapped around the gas giant Yavin, they saw a strange moon-like sphere in the distance.

The Death Star.

Each pilot in Red Squadron and Gold Squadron had a comm-unit designation. Luke's designation was Red Five. Even though he knew the names of only a few other pilots, he felt a strong bond with every one of them. They were all brave men and women, united by their willingness to put their lives on the line against the Empire.

It's a good thing everyone isn't like Han Solo, Luke thought bitterly. He tried to shake off his disappointment. *Maybe I'm wrong. Maybe I haven't seen the last of Han.*

Over his helmet's headset, Luke heard Red Leader – Garven Dreis – say, *"All wings report in."*

"Red Ten standing by."

"Red Seven standing by."

"Red Three standing by." Luke thought, *That's Biggs.*

"Red Six standing by." That's Jek Porkins. Luke had been introduced to the burly, bearded pilot just before the mission briefing.

"Red Nine standing by."

"Red Two standing by." Wedge.

"Red Eleven standing by."

"Red Five standing by," Luke said. In the astromech socket behind his cockpit, R2-D2 swivelled his head and beeped.

After the other X-wing pilots reported in, Red Leader ordered, *"Lock S-foils in attack position."*

Staying in formation, Red Squadron unfolded their starfighters' wings and locked them into the "X" position. As they neared the Death Star, the fighters began to shudder, and the pilots bounced in their cockpits.

"We're passing through their magnetic field," Red Leader announced. *"Hold tight!"*

Luke concentrated on the incoming Death Star. Red Leader ordered, *"Switch your deflectors on. Double front!"* Luke and the other pilots adjusted the controls on their fighters' shields.

The Death Star now loomed large before the

approaching starfighters. The gargantuan space station's surface was half in shadow, and the shadowed area sparkled with thousands of lights, like a planetary city at night when viewed from space. Watching the Death Star fill his X-wing's cockpit window, Wedge gasped, *"Look at the size of that thing!"*

"Cut the chatter, Red Two," Red Leader said. *"Accelerate to attack speed."* As the starfighters increased velocity, he announced, *"This is it, boys!"* The X-wings angled to fly low over the Death Star's trench.

From his Y-wing, Dutch Vander said, *"Red Leader, this is Gold Leader."*

"I copy, Gold Leader," Red Leader answered via his headset.

Gold Leader said, *"We're starting for the target shaft now."*

"We're in position," Red Leader reported. *"I'm going to cut across the axis and try and draw their fire."*

Red Leader, his wingman and two other X-wings peeled off and dived toward the Death Star's surface. The space station's large turbo-powered laser gun emplacements became visible, and the guns rotated and fired green laserbolts at the rebel fighters.

On Yavin 4, the rebel pilots' comm transmissions were broadcast over the war room's intercom. Leia and C-3PO listened as Wedge said, *"Heavy fire, boss! Twenty-three degrees."*

Red Leader answered, *"I see it. Stay low."*

Leia wondered how Luke was doing. She looked to an illuminated tactical screen, found the blip that represented the position of his X-wing over the Death Star, and kept her eyes on the blip.

From his cockpit, Luke saw Wedge manoeuvre his starfighter toward the Death Star. Luke said into his comm, "This is Red Five! I'm going in!"

Luke raced down toward the space station. Laserbolts streaked from his X-wing's cannons, creating a huge fireball explosion on the station's surface. Suddenly, Luke realised he was travelling too fast to avoid the rising flames.

Seeing Luke's situation, Biggs shouted, *"Luke, pull out!"*

Luke pulled hard on the controls and his fighter ascended rapidly through the fire. Glancing out his cockpit window, he could see fresh scorch marks on the leading edges of his wings.

Biggs asked, *"Are you all right?"*

"I got a little cooked, but I'm OK," Luke told him.

They resumed strafing the Death Star's surface with laserbolts.

✦

Alarms sounded and red lights flashed within the Death Star's corridor. As stormtroopers and droids rushed to their stations, only Darth Vader appeared to remain calm amidst the chaotic activity.

A black-uniformed Imperial officer ran up to Vader. "We count thirty rebel ships, Lord Vader. But they're so small, they're evading our turbolasers!"

"We'll have to destroy them ship to ship," Vader said. "Get the crews to their fighters."

Red Leader flew his X-wing through a heavy hail of flak. *"Watch yourself!"* he cautioned the other pilots. *"There's a lot of fire coming from the right side of that deflector tower."*

Luke sighted the deflector tower and said, "I'm on it."

Biggs said, *"I'm going in. Cover me, Porkins!"*

"I'm right with you, Red Three," answered Porkins.

Biggs and Porkins angled toward the tower and fired. There was an eruption of flames from the tower's side, but the Imperials responded with a barrage of laserfire. Porkins realised he was heading straight into the barrage and said, *"I've got a problem here."*

Biggs shouted, *"Eject!"*

"I can hold it," Porkins said, angling his ship in an attempt to avoid the criss-crossing laserbolts that

streaked from the station. He really thought he could make it.

Biggs saw otherwise and yelled, *"Pull out!"*

"No, I'm all right," Porkins said just before his fighter took a direct hit. His cockpit filled with smoke. Then his ship exploded, and Porkins was gone.

Grand Moff Tarkin watched the battle as it was displayed on a monitor in the Death Star control room. On the intercom, a voice announced, *"The rebel base will be in firing range in seven minutes."*

From Tarkin's perspective, the rebel starfighters were nothing but a slight annoyance. He couldn't imagine they would accomplish anything more than marring the surface of his space station. Still, if there were any rebel pilots left after the destruction of Yavin 4, he would make them pay for the damage.

With their lives.

Luke was still flying low over the Death Star's surface when he heard Ben's voice again. The Jedi said, *"Luke, trust your feelings."*

Luke tapped his fingers against the side of his helmet. *Nothing wrong with my headset. I wish I knew what Ben meant. Right now, my only feelings are for blowing up this space station!* He squeezed his triggers and his cannons launched more laserbolts into the Death Star, then he streaked away from the explosions.

Luke was preparing for another attack when he heard a rebel base control officer's voice on his headset. The control officer said, *"Squad leaders, we've picked up a new group of signals. Enemy fighters coming your way."*

"My scope's negative," Luke reported. "I don't see anything."

"Pick up your visual scanning," Red Leader advised.

In their respective cockpits, Luke and Biggs turned their heads to look outside their windows, searching for any sight of incoming Imperial fighters. Red Leader spotted the ships first and warned, *"Here they come."*

There were six TIE fighters. Flying in an incredibly tight formation, they raced toward the rebel ships, then fanned out to pursue individual targets.

"Watch it!" Red Leader shouted to a young pilot named John D., whose comm-unit designation was Red Four. *"You've got one on your tail."*

John D. tried to evade the TIE fighter's laserfire, but ultimately failed. His X-wing shattered and exploded, scattering debris in all directions.

Red Leader visually scanned the other fighters in his squadron. *"Biggs! You've picked one up. Watch it!"*

"I can't see it!" Biggs answered. He sent his X-wing into a series of tight swerves but the TIE fighter followed

each evasive manoeuvre. Green laserfire whizzed past Biggs. *"They're on me tight. I can't shake him . . ."*

"I'll be right there," Luke said, angling his X-wing to pursue the TIE fighter that was right on Biggs' tail. Glancing at his targeting computer, Luke locked the target into his sights and fired. The TIE fighter exploded in a mass of flames.

Luke thought, *I don't know how much longer we can keep this up. If the Death Star deploys even more TIE fighters, we'll really be in for it!*

Darth Vader strode purposefully down a Death Star corridor and came to a stop before two black-clad Imperial TIE fighter pilots. Like their stormtrooper counterparts, the Imperial pilots were entirely without fear.

Vader said, "Several fighters have broken off from the main group. Come with me!" He headed for a door that led to a hangar. The two pilots followed.

On Yavin 4, Leia and C-3PO continued listening to the transmissions from the rebel pilots. Over the intercom, Biggs said, *"Pull in! Luke . . . pull in!"*

Then Wedge said, *"Watch your back, Luke!"*

Leia tried to visualise what was happening over the Death Star, and trembled.

+

In his cockpit, Luke heard Wedge say, *"Watch your back! Fighters above you, coming in!"*

Luke angled away from the Death Star's surface until he spotted the tailing TIE fighter. The Imperial pilot fired and scored a hit on Luke's X-wing, striking the port upper thrust engine. The X-wing bounced hard and flames streamed from the damaged engine.

"I'm hit, but not bad," Luke announced as he took evasive action. "Artoo, see what you can do with it. Hang on back there."

R2-D2 rotated his dome to extend a repair arm to the port engine. The brave astromech ignored the green laserfire that whizzed past the X-wing.

Red Leader lost sight of Luke. *"Can you see Red Five?"* he asked his squadron.

Red Ten – a young man named Theron Nett – answered, *"There's a heavy fire zone on this side. Red Five, where are you?"*

Luke was still trying to evade the same TIE fighter that had struck his X-wing. Soaring away from the Death Star, Luke said, "I can't shake him!"

"I'm on him, Luke!" Wedge called in. *"Hold on!"* Wedge dived toward Luke and the TIE fighter.

Luke increased speed, but the TIE fighter clung to his trail. Growing frantic as he waited for Wedge to come to his aid, Luke suddenly realised he'd lost sight of Biggs. Luke said, "Blast it! Biggs, where are you?"

Biggs was rapidly racing to Luke's position, but Wedge got there first. In a daring manoeuvre, Wedge guided his X-wing straight for the cockpit window of Luke's pursuer. Wedge fired his cannons and the TIE fighter's spherical command pod exploded into space dust. Because of his velocity, Wedge was unable to pull out, but he quickly angled his X-wing to fly through the fiery explosion, narrowly missing the two hexagonal wings that were all that remained of the destroyed TIE fighter.

"Thanks, Wedge," Luke said, breathing a sigh of relief.

"Good shooting, Wedge!" Biggs chimed in.

As Luke readjusted his controls, he heard the voice of Y-wing pilot Dutch Vander speak over his headset: *"Red Leader, this is Gold Leader. We're starting our attack run."*

Red Leader replied, *"I copy, Gold Leader. Move into position."*

While Gold Leader and two other Y-wings descended to the enormous space station's trench, Darth Vader and his two wingmen piloted their TIE fighters out of a Death Star hangar and into space. Vader's ship was a TIE Advanced x1 Prototype with an elongated rear deck and matching solar arrays that bent in toward the central command pod.

"Stay in attack formation!" Vader said into his fighter's comlink as he led his wingmen to the rebel ships.

Gold Leader adjusted his scopes as he guided Gold Two and Gold Five down to the Death Star's equatorial trench, en route to the vulnerable exhaust port. Seeing the readout for their target on the nav computer, Gold Leader said, "The exhaust port is marked and locked in!"

Three Y-wings swooped down into the high-walled trench. Gold Five - an older pilot named Davish "Pops" Krail - took the lead position. Gold Leader was Krail's starboard wingman, and Gold Two - a young pilot named Dex Tiree - was his port wingman.

Imperial cannons were along the upper edges of the trench walls, and larger cannons were mounted atop angular towers on the Death Star's surface. The cannons fired green lasers and flak exploded around the three Y-wings.

Gold Leader said, "Switch all power to front deflector screens. Switch all power to front deflector screens." Maintaining a high speed, the pilots dipped and shifted to avoid being hit. Gold Leader tried to count the streaks of laserfire and asked, "How many guns do you think, Gold Five?"

"Say about twenty guns," Gold Five answered. *"Some on the surface, some on the towers."*

✦

The Y-wing pilots' communications were broadcast over the loudspeaker at the rebel base. There, Leia cringed when she heard the announcement over the loudspeaker: "*Death Star will be in range in five minutes.*"

The rebel pilots were also aware of the limited time they had left, but if they were nervous, none of them showed it. Gold Leader's voice remained steady as he said, "Switch to targeting computer."

Inside the cockpit of each Y-wing, the targeting computer scopes automatically adjusted before the pilots so they could monitor their progress to the target site. Laserfire continued to whiz past the three fighters.

"*Computer's locked,*" Gold Two confirmed as his fighter flew through bursts of flak. A beeping sound accompanied a blinking blip on his targeting scope, and he added, "*Getting a signal.*"

Suddenly, the barrage of Imperial laserfire came to an abrupt end. Baffled, Gold Two said, "*The guns . . . they've stopped!*"

Even though the three pilots were still travelling at high speed, the trench seemed eerily calm. Gold Five glanced out of his cockpit window and said, "*Stabilise your rear deflectors. Watch for enemy fighters.*"

Gold Leader saw the three TIE fighters first. "They're coming in! Three marks at two ten."

+

The three marks were Darth Vader and his two wingmen. With inhuman precision, the Imperial fighters hurtled into the Death Star trench to arrive behind the Y-wings.

"I'll take them myself," Vader said into his comlink. "Cover me."

"Yes, sir," answered an Imperial pilot.

Vader lined up Gold Two in his targeting computer, then pressed the trigger on his fighter's control stick. Laserfire streaked out from Vader's ship and Gold Two's Y-wing exploded in a blinding flash.

Gold Leader saw the explosion - saw his friend Tiree die in a split second - and began to panic. "It's no good," he said into his comlink. "I can't manoeuvre!"

"Stay on target!" Gold Five said, trying to keep Gold Leader calm.

Gold Leader tried to adjust his targeting computer and said, "We're too close."

"Stay on target!" Gold Five repeated calmly.

"Loosen up!" Gold Leader snapped.

Darth Vader adjusted his own targeting computer. He locked onto Gold Leader's ship, then pressed the control stick's trigger. The Y-wing exploded, killing Dutch Vander and throwing debris in all directions.

Pops Krail was close to the target area, but with

three TIE fighters on his tail, he knew he wouldn't last much longer if he remained in the trench. Guiding his Y-wing up and out of the trench, he said, "Gold Five to Red Leader - lost Tiree, lost Dutch. They came from behind -" Before Pops could finish, one of his engines exploded. Darth Vader's TIE fighter had followed Pops out of the trench and fired a devastating blast at the Y-wing. The starfighter blazed out of control, exploded, and Pops was gone.

In the Death Star control room, Grand Moff Tarkin's aide, Chief Bast, left a computer console to report to his leader. Tarkin stood before the large viewscreen, watching the Death Star's progress through space, and waiting for the moment that the planet Yavin no longer obscured Yavin 4.

Chief Bast said, "We've analysed their attack, sir, and there is a danger. Should I have your ship standing by?"

"Evacuate?" Tarkin said, outraged. "In our moment of triumph? I think you overestimate their chances!"

Tarkin returned his attention to the viewscreen. Over the Death Star's intercom, a voice announced, "*Rebel base, three minutes and closing.*"

CHAPTER 15

THIRTY rebel pilots had travelled in their starfighters from Yavin 4 to the Death Star. Standing in the rebel base war room, Leia looked at a tactical monitor and saw that only about six X-wings and a single Y-wing remained engaged in the battle. One of the X-wings was Luke's, but with less than three minutes until the Death Star entered firing range of Yavin 4, it was hard for Leia to remain hopeful for any rebel's future.

From over the war room's loudspeaker came X-wing pilot Garven Dreis's voice: "*Red boys, this is Red Leader. Rendezvous at mark six point one.*"

"*This is Red Two,*" Wedge answered. "*Flying toward you.*"

"*Red Three, standing by,*" said Biggs.

Leia knew Luke was Red Five. The two remaining X-wing pilots carried the comm-unit designations of Red Ten and Red Twelve. Near Leia, General Dodonna examined the tactical screen and said into his comm,

"Red Leader, this is Base One. Keep half your group out of range for the next run."

"Copy, Base One," Red Leader said. Addressing his pilots, he continued, "Luke, take Red Two and Three. Hold up here and wait for my signal to start your run."

Luke got the message. If Red Leader failed to reach the exhaust port, it would be up to Luke - with Wedge and Biggs as his wingmen - to enter the trench and make one final attempt at the target.

In his cockpit, Red Leader glanced around to watch for the TIE fighters. Beads of sweat broke out across his forehead but he dismissed the nervous reflex and tightened his grip on his control stick. "This is it!" he said, and threw his X-wing down into the Death Star's trench. Red Ten and Red Twelve followed him.

The Death Star cannons fired at the three X-wings as they raced through the high-walled trench. As laserfire streaked past them, Red Ten quickly consulted his targeting scope, then tried to sight a cannon tower that would visually indicate the target site. He said, *"We should be able to see it by now."*

The Imperial cannons ceased firing. Red Leader said, "Keep your eyes open for those fighters!"

Red Ten said, *"There's too much interference!"* Indeed, the X-wing's sensors had been designed for travelling through space, not for speeding through a space station trench, and it was difficult for Red Ten to identify the blips on his scopes. Red Ten said into his comm, *"Red Five, can you see them from where you are?"*

From above the trench, Luke answered, *"No sign of any – wait!"* He saw the three TIE fighters, and said, *"Coming in point three five."*

Red Ten looked up and said, *"I see them."*

Sunlight flared off the solar arrays of the three TIE fighters as they dived in a tight formation for the trench. Advancing on the three X-wings, Darth Vader was surprised to feel a twinge of anticipation. He was looking forward to killing more rebel pilots.

Red Leader blocked out thoughts of the incoming enemy fighters and displayed calm as he adjusted his targeting computer. He said, "I'm in range." On his targeting scope, the blinking blip indicated he was closing in on the Death Star's thermal exhaust port. "Target's coming up!" he announced. "Just hold them off for a few seconds."

Since the X-wings were without tail guns, all Red Ten and Red Twelve could do was increase power to their rear deflector shields and manoeuvre to defend Red Leader against a rear attack.

From behind, Darth Vader said into his comm, *"Close up formation."* His wingmen complied.

Red Leader lined up the target in the crosshairs of his scope. "Almost there!" he said.

Darth Vader's targeting computer locked onto Red Twelve's X-wing. Vader pressed his control stick's trigger and his cannons spat green laserfire. The X-wing exploded and crashed against the walls of the trench.

The power of the blast nearly sent Red Ten out of control too. Struggling to stay on course behind Red Leader, Red Ten said into his comm, *"You'd better let her loose."*

But Red Leader wasn't ready yet. All his attention was concentrated on his targeting scope, waiting for the right moment to fire his X-wing's proton torpedoes.

Red Ten said, *"They're right behind me."*

"Almost there!" Red Leader said.

"I can't hold them!" Red Ten yelled. He looked to his left, trying to find the position of the TIE fighters.

Vader coolly pressed the trigger on his control stick. His well-aimed shot smashed into the X-wing, and Red Ten's cockpit filled with fire and smoke. An instant later, the X-wing exploded.

Red Leader grimly watched the target line up in his scope's crosshairs, then he fired. As the two proton torpedoes zoomed down the trench, he yelled, "It's away!" He pulled up into a rapid climb just before a huge explosion billowed out of the trench.

In the rebel base, everyone held their breath as they

waited to hear the pilot's transmissions over the loudspeaker. Red Nine exclaimed, *"It's a hit!"*

"Negative," Red Leader said with finality. *"Negative! It didn't go in, just impacted on the surface."*

The announcement stunned everyone in the rebel war room. Leia wished General Dodonna would assure her that they still had a chance, but Dodonna didn't say a word.

Luke looked down from his cockpit and sighted Red Leader's ship. The TIE fighters had followed Red Leader out of the trench and were moving up fast behind him. Luke said, "Red Leader, we're right above you. Turn to point . . . oh-five; we'll cover for you."

"Stay there," Red Leader said. Looking nervously through his cockpit window, he added, *"I just lost my starboard engine. Get set up for your attack run."*

Darth Vader fired at Red Leader's X-wing. The X-wing caught fire and Garven Dreis screamed as his ship plummeted to the Death Star. Luke watched helplessly as the X-wing crashed and exploded.

No time to mourn, Luke thought. *Now it's up to me, Biggs and Wedge.*

Grand Moff Tarkin cast a sinister eye at the Death Star control room's viewscreen. Over the intercom, a voice announced, *"Rebel base, one minute and closing."*

+

Speeding over the Death Star's surface, Luke said, "Biggs, Wedge, let's close it up. We're going in. We're going in full throttle. That ought to keep those fighters off our back."

Wedge said, *"Right with you, boss."*

Concerned, Biggs said, *"Luke, at that speed, will you be able to pull out in time?"*

"It'll be just like Beggar's Canyon back home," Luke told his old friend.

Wedge and Biggs followed Luke down into the Death Star's trench. They unleashed a barrage of laserfire at the space station, and the Imperial cannons returned fire.

As Luke raced ahead, Biggs said, *"We'll stay back far enough to cover you."*

Wedge said, *"My scope shows the tower, but I can't see the exhaust port! Are you sure the computer can hit it?"*

Luke heard the question but was momentarily distracted by a Death Star cannon that slowly rotated and pumped laserbolts at the X-wings. "Watch yourself!" Luke said. "Increase speed full throttle!"

"What about that tower?" Wedge said.

"You worry about those fighters!" Luke said. "I'll worry about the tower!"

Imperial laserfire nicked one of Luke's wings and he

had to struggle with his controls to steady the starfighter's flight. "Artoo," he said into his comm, "that stabiliser's broken loose again. See if you can't lock it down!"

As R2-D2 extended his repair arm once more, the Death Star's cannons ceased firing. Flying behind Luke's X-wing, Wedge looked up and saw the enemy pilots making their approach. Wedge announced, *"Fighters. Coming in, point three."*

The three TIE fighters swooped into the trench. Luke focused on his targeting scope, which had just marked off the distance to the target. The TIE fighters zoomed closer to the X-wings. Darth Vader fired.

"I'm hit!" Wedge shouted as his ship was blasted from behind. *"I can't stay with you!"*

"Get clear, Wedge," Luke said. "You can't do any more good back there!"

"Sorry!" Wedge said as he pulled his crippled X-wing up and out of the trench.

Darth Vader sensed one of his wingmen wanted to pursue the fleeing X-wing. *"Let him go!"* Vader commanded. *"Stay on the leader!"* The TIE fighters maintained their tight formation as they accelerated.

Biggs gazed back at the incoming TIE fighters. *"Hurry, Luke,"* he said with worry. *"They're coming in much faster this time. We can't hold them!"*

Luke glanced back from his cockpit and said, "Artoo, try and increase the power!"

R2-D2 worked frantically on the engines. Swivelling his dome, he saw the TIE fighters were gaining fast on Biggs' X-wing.

Luke looked into his targeting scope. Over his headset, he heard Biggs say, *"Hurry up, Luke!"*

Biggs glanced at the TIE fighters and moved in to cover for Luke. Darth Vader gained on Biggs. Biggs shouted, *"Wait!"*

Vader fired. Luke looked back and saw the X-wing that carried his best friend suddenly explode into a million flaming bits.

Biggs!

The TIE fighters kept coming. As Luke's eyes watered, his anger grew.

Inside the Death Star, Grand Moff Tarkin felt nothing but satisfaction when the announcement came over the intercom: *"Rebel base, thirty seconds and closing."*

"I'm on the leader," Darth Vader told his wingmen as he adjusted his targeting computer. The three TIE fighters charged after the lone X-wing that remained in the trench.

✦

At the rebel base, Princess Leia glanced at C-3PO. Nervous, the droid said, "Hang on, Artoo!"

Luke adjusted the lens on his targeting scope. The exhaust port was still some distance ahead, and the TIE fighters were coming in fast from behind. *I don't think I'm going to make it.*

Then, he heard Ben's voice: "*Use the Force, Luke.*"

Luke looked outside the cockpit. *Ben?*

Ben's voice said, "*Let go, Luke.*"

Suddenly, time seemed to slow down. Luke felt not as if he were racing through the Death Star's trench at full throttle, but rather that the trench was flowing past and around him. He was aware of the pursuing TIE fighters and the weapon-laden trench walls, but he no longer felt threatened by them. He was in control, and he was not afraid.

Darth Vader sensed the change that swept over the pilot in the remaining X-wing. As Vader tried to lock onto the rebel starfighter with his targeting computer, he said, "The Force is strong in this one!"

Luke looked at his own targeting scope.

Ben's voice said, "*Luke, trust me.*"

Luke reached to his control panel and pressed a button. The targeting scope retracted and moved away from his helmet.

Luke's action was detected by the controllers at the

rebel base. A controller announced, *"His computer's off."* Addressing Luke directly, he said, *"Luke, you switched off your targeting computer. What's wrong?"*

"Nothing," Luke answered as he stayed on course for his target. "I'm all right." *I don't need the targeting computer. All I have to do is get a bit closer to the exhaust port. I can do it! I know I can do it . . .*

Behind Luke, R2-D2 rotated his dome again to look at the incoming TIE fighters. The central TIE fighter fired a burst of laserbolts at the X-wing, and the astromech was engulfed by crackling laserfire. R2-D2 screeched, then went silent.

"I've lost Artoo!" Luke shouted.

C-3PO heard Luke over the war room loudspeaker, and the golden droid looked to Princess Leia. Like the other rebels, she had her eyes fixed on the tactical monitor. The controller announced, "The Death Star has cleared the planet. The Death Star has cleared the planet."

There was a simultaneous announcement in the Death Star control room: "Rebel base, in range."

Tarkin turned to an Imperial officer and said, "You may fire when ready."

The officer pressed a button on an illuminated control panel. "Commence primary ignition."

+

While the Imperial soldiers readied the Death Star's superlaser, Darth Vader's targeting computer locked on to Luke's X-wing. Taking careful aim, Vader said, "I have you now." He pressed the trigger.

Suddenly, an unexpected blast of laserfire angled down into the trench and struck the TIE fighter that had been travelling alongside Vader's starboard stern. The TIE fighter exploded. Vader exclaimed, "What?" He glanced up to locate the unknown attacker.

It was the *Millennium Falcon*.

"Yahoo!" Han Solo hollered as he descended rapidly from above, guiding the *Falcon* on what looked like a collision course for the two TIE fighters.

Intending to warn Darth Vader, the startled surviving Imperial wingman cried, "Look out!" But the sight of the oncoming Corellian freighter caused the wingman to panic, and he veered radically to one side and smashed against Vader's TIE fighter. The impact sent Vader's fighter spinning up and out of the trench, while the wingman crashed into the wall and exploded. Vader fought to regain control of his fighter but it continued to tumble across space, leaving the Death Star behind.

The *Falcon* pulled out of its steep dive and Han said into his comm, "You're all clear, kid. Now let's blow this thing up and go home!"

Luke looked up and smiled, then concentrated on

the exhaust port. *I can sense the target. It's right in front of me. I cannot miss.*

Luke fired the proton torpedoes. The twin projectiles streaked away from his X-wing, carrying their payload of high-yield warheads. Both torpedoes plunged down into the thermal exhaust port, and Luke – travelling at an almost sickening speed – pulled up and out of the trench and accelerated to catch up with the *Millennium Falcon*, Wedge's X-wing and a single Y-wing, which were already speeding away from the Death Star.

Inside the space station, the superlaser was finally ready to be fired. Grand Moff Tarkin's eyes remained fixed on the viewscreen as an Imperial controller announced, "Stand by."

The three rebel starfighters and the *Falcon* were barely out of the danger zone when the Death Star exploded in an immense, blinding flash. From a distance, the blast resembled a small supernova.

"Great shot, kid," Han said into his comm. "That was one in a million."

Luke let out a deep breath and relaxed. Ben's voice said, *"Remember, the Force will be with you . . . always."*

Luke smiled all the way back to Yavin 4.

EPILOGUE

DARTH Vader regained a measure of control of his damaged TIE fighter. As he programmed a distress call to the Imperial Star Destroyer *Devastator*, he was not preoccupied about how he would explain the loss of the Death Star to the Emperor. Tarkin had been responsible for the space station and its vulnerabilities, and the rebels had been more cunning than anyone had anticipated. There was really nothing more to say.

But there were plenty of other things to think about. Before Vader had been knocked out of the trench, he'd recognised the Corellian freighter as the same ship that had delivered Ben Kenobi to the Death Star, reportedly from Tatooine. Vader wondered why Kenobi had been on Tatooine, and how long he'd been there.

Then Vader thought of the last X-wing pilot in the trench. *He was so strong with the Force.*

Vader wouldn't rest until he learned the truth.

After landing in the main hangar at the rebel base on Yavin 4, Luke climbed out of his battered X-wing to be greeted by a throng of cheering rebels. As he descended the ladder beside his ship, he searched the crowd for one face in particular, and then he saw her.

"Luke!" Leia shouted as she rushed to him. She threw her arms around his neck and they danced in a circle. As Luke span, he saw C-3PO make his way through the crowd to stand beside the X-wing, then saw Han and Chewbacca come running toward them.

"Hey! Hey!" Han said as he embraced Luke.

"I knew you'd come back!" Luke said. "I just knew it!"

Han playfully shoved Luke's face and laughed. "Well, I wasn't gonna let you get all the credit and take all the reward."

Leia beamed at Han and said, "Hey, I knew there was more to you than money."

A maintenance crew had removed R2-D2 from the X-wing and lowered him down to the hangar floor. Seeing the astromech's scorched body, Luke said, "Oh, no!"

"Oh, my!" C-3PO cried. "Artoo! Can you hear me? Say something!" When no reply came from R2-D2, C-3PO looked to the maintenance crew and said, "You can repair him, can't you?"

One of the technicians said, "We'll get to work on him right away."

"You must repair him!" C-3PO said. Turning to Luke, C-3PO added, "Sir, if any of my circuits or gears will help, I'll gladly donate them."

"He'll be all right," Luke said with great assurance. He had good reason to feel confident. He was no longer a kid with no future on a desert planet.

He was the pilot who'd just blown up the Death Star.

The next day, trumpets sounded over the great temple. In the expansive ruins of the temple's high-ceilinged main throne room, hundreds of uniformed rebel troops stood at attention and faced a long aisle. The aisle extended to the far end of the chamber and ended at steps that led up to an elevated level, upon which stood Princess Leia, General Dodonna and the other Alliance leaders.

Luke, Han and Chewbacca entered the throne room. Luke wore an Alliance-issue yellow flight jacket over a black tunic, brown trousers and dark leather boots. Han wore his own clothes, including a clean shirt he'd been saving for a special occasion. Chewbacca wore his bandolier.

The Wookiee followed the two men up the aisle, passing the silent troops as they marched solemnly toward the princess. When the trio arrived at the steps, Chewbacca glanced aside and barked at the troops. As if in response, the troops turned simultaneously on their heels to face the rebel leaders.

Luke and Han ascended the steps and stopped just

below Leia. Chewbacca was uncomfortable with the situation and remained on a lower step, behind Han.

Princess Leia wore a white gown and a silver necklace and bracelet. She looked to Han and Luke. Luke was unable to maintain a serious expression and broke out in a big smile. Leia smiled in return.

General Dodonna handed a gold medallion to Leia. Han bowed as the princess placed the medallion around his neck. As he rose, Han winked at Leia.

Luke glanced over to C-3PO, who stood beside the rebel leaders. The protocol droid was gleaming from head to toe, and appeared very proud. Luke nodded to acknowledge C-3PO, then returned his attention to Leia and the ceremony. He lowered his head, and Leia placed a medallion around his neck too.

Then both Han and Luke bowed to Leia, and a happy beeping sound came from beside C-3PO. It was R2 D2. The astromech had been completely refurbished, and looked better than he had when he'd been brand new. R2-D2 wobbled back and forth with excitement, causing all to grin.

Luke, Han and Chewbacca turned to face the assembled troops, and the ancient temple was suddenly filled with loud cheers and applause. Chewbacca surveyed the crowd and growled.

Even though friends had been lost, and the battle against the Empire was far from over, the fact remained that a small band of heroes had destroyed the Death Star against impossible odds. For that, the rebels found cause to celebrate. And they did.